Sharon,
Thank you for the support!
Enjoy the story!
♡ Deanne

To Live Without Knowing

Deanne Rupert

Copyright © 2017 Deanne Rupert

All rights reserved

ISBN: 1978337477
ISBN-13: 978-1978337473

For anyone who has ever felt unwelcome in their hometown. May you one day find your home, wherever, whatever, or whomever it may be.

One

September 2017 – Maine

The sun had barely come up over the horizon when the first beachcombers began trickling out onto the sands of Ferry Beach in Saco, Maine. Each of them dragged their umbrellas, coolers, and various beach bags behind them in their desperate attempt to get the best spot available. Summers in Maine didn't usually last long, and everyone wanted to squeeze out as much beach time as they possibly could, especially since it was Labor Day weekend and the official last Saturday of the summer according to locals. Another few weeks or so, and the mercury would already begin to dip, making sitting out on the beach in a bathing suit incredibly uncomfortable, if not impossible. Sweatshirts and winter coats would once again be pulled out of the back of closets, and the beach gear would be stowed away in garages and basements.

    Jaime Strait was just about finished her morning run along the water as the early birds were beginning to set up their umbrellas and shake out their beach towels covered in palm trees and Disney characters. Morning beach runs had become a somewhat of a ritual for Jaime since she moved to Maine seven years prior. It was a little cooler by the water, especially before the sun showed itself, but running on the beach was much more peaceful than running on the sidewalk next to the busy road. Now that summer was beginning to wind down the beach would be mostly empty in the coming weeks, something Jaime was very much looking forward to. She loved living in Maine, but wasn't a huge fan of all the tourists that made the journey north in the summer. On more than one occasion during her morning runs

Jaime had to weave around beach chairs, and avoid wayward football and frisbees tossed around by college students. One of whom had affectionately called Jaime 'bro' after she threw a perfect spiral back to him.

Maine had become her home these last seven years. Jaime had moved two weeks after finishing college at Penn State. She knew while still in school she hadn't wanted to move back to her small Pennsylvania town she was originally from. There were too many ghosts there. Jaime knew with a journalism degree she could go almost anywhere, so that's where she applied for jobs. Jaime reckoned she had sent out close to seventy-five applications during her last semester of college. They went to every corner of the continental U.S. and even put a handful in for a few places in Canada. The first place she heard back from was a magazine based out of Portland, Maine called *The Way*

Life Should Be. A small periodical that covered what it was like to live in and visit Maine. Each issue showcased typical Maine things like hunting moose, picking blueberries, eating lobster, snowshoeing, and a variety of other topics. During her spring break week of senior year, she made the trip from Pennsylvania to Maine for an interview, and immediately fell in love with Maine and its people. She loved the accent of its residents, even if she could only understand about every third word at first. She loved the smell of the salt water and the cry of the gulls as they searched for their next meal. It felt like a completely different world than the small, farm town she had grown up in and she loved that.

    Jaime had the job offer before the interview was even done, and something to look forward to after graduation. Her parents were thrilled when she arrived home with the news of a job, but Jaime could tell that they were still sad she would be leaving home. Her mom gripped her tight in a hug and squealed her congratulations, but Jaime could still see the tears pooling in her eyes. She didn't allow them to fall, but they remained visible just behind her thin rimmed glasses. They hadn't expected Jaime to stay in Pennsylvania after college, but that didn't stop them from wishing for it, even if they could understand why she needed to leave so badly. Their town was exactly that – theirs – and it hadn't been a home for Jaime for a very long time.

Jaime pulled up to her apartment complex after her run that morning and immediately noticed a new hunter green Jeep Wrangler sitting in the lot. There were only ten tenants who lived in the complex, the landlord being one, and Jaime had catalogued each of their cars quickly in her mind. She was just about to brush it off when she noticed the faded Grateful Dead sticker in the back window. She knew the person who drove this car. Hell, she had spent many a Friday and Saturday night riding shotgun in this car. She was even there when that sticker was carefully placed in that back window. *Stop shaking the Jeep!* She remembered laughing as the owner of the Jeep tried to put it on perfect with no air bubbles.

Suddenly, her mind flashed back to fifteen years ago when she was just fourteen. Two years before this Jeep had even come into her life. No, she chastised herself, no fucking way. Don't even go there. But deep down inside she already knew why this Jeep was sitting outside her apartment. Her stomach twisted, and she had to grip the steering wheel until the cramp passed. Something very bad has happened.

11

The apartment complex's double set of automatic doors slid open as Jaime approached from the parking lot. Goosebumps began to rise on her arms as she entered the lobby. She wasn't sure if they were from the air conditioner or the thought of who/what was waiting for her inside. On one side of the lobby sat two couches and an armchair surrounding a coffee table. Across the room was a little breakfast bar that was stocked every morning with coffee, creamer, sugar, tea, muffins, and granola bars. Geraldine, the woman who ran the front desk made sure everything was always fresh and hot each morning when she arrived.

It was at the breakfast bar where Jaime's suspicions were confirmed. Pouring a fresh cup of coffee stood a man who towered over everything. Seeing this man standing where he was, in a lobby was filled with furniture and decorations that one might consider old fashioned, was almost comical to Jaime. He was clad in jeans, biker boots, and a flannel shirt. Jaime surmised he probably had a band shirt on underneath the flannel, Metallica or AC/DC, perhaps. His hair was a little longer than seven years ago, but it was still shaggy and windswept. Everything about him was a stark contrast to the sea foam green walls, the light gray and blue couches, the nautical themed pictures on the wall. The only thing Jaime found out of the ordinary about him was the shoulder bag that hung off his right shoulder.

"Please don't tell me you drove here on no sleep," Jaime called out in order to get his attention, smiling in spite of her anxiety.

Her voice startled him at first, but then he turned and her anxiety was gone. There was still fresh stubble and a toothy grin on his face just like she remembered. She glanced down at his t-shirt, and found her smile widening.

Metallica. S*ome things never change*, she thought wistfully. Jaime hadn't stepped foot in her hometown in seven years, but Flynn was still her best friend.

He took two steps towards her and she met him in the middle of the lobby. Their arms tangled around each other, and the giant swept Jaime up off the ground easily, crushing her smaller body tightly to his far larger one. The fact that she was still sweaty from her run, didn't seem to faze him for a second.

"Fuck, I missed you." He rasped, tickling her ear with his warm breath. Suddenly she was fourteen again and her best friend was hugging her after a rough day at school, or after Flynn had led the boys' basketball team to the state playoffs. "Social media and texting aren't the same as being here in person."

"I know. Flynn, look, I'm so sorry I haven't been home in so long," she began only to be cut off by him.

"No. No way do you ever have to apologize for not coming back to that shithole." His mouth transformed from a soft smile to a snarl. If Jaime hadn't of known him so well, she almost would have thought he was angry with her. If Jaime didn't know why he was here before, she knew now.

He set her back down on the ground, and ran a hand through his hair, a nervous tic of his he used to do all the time that Jaime picked up on immediately.

"Something's happened, hasn't it," she spat out. Not exactly how she wanted this to go, but the wheels were already turning.

Flynn's eyes shifted nervously around the lobby before they finally found Jaime's. *Shit. How bad could it be?*

15

"Yeah," he breathed out. "Yeah, something's happened."

Jaime nodded once, and then spoke again.

"Come on, let's go up to my apartment where we can talk. But first, I need a shower and some coffee."

Jaime padded out of her bedroom clad in a pair of purple basketball shorts and a tank top after her quicker than usual shower. She had combed her wet hair out, and her usually wavy blonde hair hung straight for the moment. She found Flynn sitting at her kitchen table with two fresh mugs of coffee sitting in front of him. He was running his hands through his hair again, but when he saw Jaime he forced his hands away from his head and smiled.

"You're still wearing those damn purple shorts?" Flynn asked shaking his head.

"Don't be hating on my shorts! How many two on two games at the Corner Street court did we win while I was wearing these shorts?"

"The only reason we won those games was because of my impeccable play in the paint."

Jaime found herself smiling in spite of the situation. It was as if seven days had passed instead of seven years. How many people had that kind of relationship with their best friend? You couldn't buy a friendship like that.

"So," Jaime said folding her legs underneath herself in the chair adjacent to Flynn's. "As happy as I am to see you, you're not here just because you missed me, are you?"

Flynn's smile fell away from his face, and his eyes hardened. He swallowed once and then spoke.

17

"It's happening again,"

Jaime's heart paused in her chest, and her mouth suddenly felt like sandpaper. Her hands gripped her mug so tight she was sure she would crush it between them.

"How do you know it's the same thing?"

"Jaime, I'm sure. I never would have come up here if I wasn't," Flynn explained. "I waited as long as I could, but I can't wait, we can't wait, any longer. Three people have already gone missing this year that I know of."

Flynn paused for a minute after this, visibly struggling with the next words he needed to voice to his best friend. He was worried how she might react. Tears he could handle. He'd seen Jaime cry a handful of times before, that was the easy one. He was terrified, however, that she would get angry and throw him out of her apartment. That she would tell him to never call, never come back. He didn't think he'd be able to live with himself if it came to that.

"Jaime, the last person to go missing was Amber."

For a split-second Jaime's face fell when she heard her childhood love, her only love, had numbered amongst those recently missing. Jaime knew that she was likely dead by now. People went missing in Hawk Ridge, Pennsylvania, and they were never heard from again. It's how things worked in their little town. She could see Amber screaming in agony, her body being twisted in different directions, and then forced herself to stop.

"When." It was as though the shock of hearing the news had robbed Jaime of her voice. She could barely get a whisper out. "When did it happen?"

"Thursday night," Flynn responded. "There was a football scrimmage at the high school, one last tune-up before the season starts next week. From what I've read in the paper and heard around town, she went to the restroom sometime in the third quarter, and then never came back."

"And I'm guessing no one saw anything, right?"

"You would be correct. Her asshat husband didn't think anything of it until the game ended, and he couldn't reach her on her cell phone. Thought maybe she just caught a ride home early with a friend, but when he couldn't find her when he got home he sounded the alarm. When I woke up yesterday morning the whole town was discussing what might have happened."

"So now what?" Jaime inquired, already knowing what Flynn was about to say.

Flynn took a deep breath, and then let it out slowly. He went to chew on his thumbnail, but caught himself. He turned his head to the side for a second, avoiding Jaime's eyes for the second time that morning, until he finally worked up the nerve to say the words that needed saying.

"I need your help. I need you to come home with me."

Two

August 2002 – Pennsylvania

Jaime sliced through the water like a hot knife cutting through butter. Her head emerged from under the water a second later, and she lazily stroked her way over to the edge of the in-ground pool. Once at the edge, she folded her arms on the cement that surrounded the pool, warmed by the August sun. She placed her chin on top of them, grinning at her companion who was sitting in a lounge chair a few feet away.

"You really should be on the swim team, you know that right?"

Jaime responded by grinning even wider, and then used her arms to lift herself up out of the water and onto the hot cement. She hurried over to the second lounge chair and slipped her feet into her flip flops. It was barely noon and the sunflower shaped thermometer hanging on the gate that ran around the pool was already reading close to one hundred degrees.

"I'm serious. You'd be faster than most of the seniors this year, as a freshman! Imagine what you could do in four years!"

Jaime shrugged and grabbed her towel.

"I'll think about it." She replied with a smirk as she continued to dry herself off. "What about you? Are you going to play soccer, Miss 3x Hawk Ridge PeeWee Soccer League MVP?"

This inquiry was met with a sigh of frustration and a scowl. She slammed the plastic water bottle she had been holding down onto the small table next to her lounge chair. Jaime suspected had it been a glass instead of a plastic bottle, Amber would be sporting several cuts along the palm of her hand.

"Not this year. My parents don't like the idea of me playing sports in high school, especially one where I'd be travelling with and undressing around other girls all the time. Of course, that's not exactly how they worded it."

Jaime raised an eyebrow at this.

"So they know about you?"

Amber let out another frustrated sigh.

"I think they suspect something, my mom especially. I have no idea how, my guess it's some kind of mom ESP or something. She's always been religious, but lately it's been over the top stuff. She's started turning the TV off if there's a gay character or a gay actor on it. She even started lighting a candle for me every week in church. Says it's because I'm starting high school this year, but I have a feeling it's for something else."

Jaime was silent for a moment, thinking over what Amber had just said.

"They have no idea we've been hanging out, do they?" She asked a little hurt.

The look on Amber's face was all the answer she needed.

"Please don't be mad at me," Amber begged. "They'd crucify me if they knew I was having you over during the day to go swimming. Being alone with another girl in her bathing suit? They'd lose their fucking minds. They'd probably immediately take me to Father Collins to be exorcised or something."

"I'm sorry you have to put up with this shit," Jamie responded. "I wish we could just leave this stupid, ass-backwards town. Go somewhere where we can be our true selves."

Amber reached out and took Jaime's hand, lacing their fingers together, a small innocent act, but had they done this anywhere else outside of Amber's backyard in town most people would have had a heart attack.

"Me fucking too. But, for now we just have to be smart about where we hang out and who we hang out with. High school doesn't last forever. Once we're eighteen, we can jet off to college and make a life for ourselves. Get ourselves a little apartment, maybe even a dog."

Jaime thought it over. Amber was right about one thing, high school doesn't last forever, but sometimes it sure felt like it would.

Three

"Flynn –."

"Wait," he interrupted. "Listen to me. I know I have no right asking you to come back to that place after everything you went through there growing up. You don't owe that place a single thing, but I need your help. Jaime, I was the only person to believe you fifteen years ago. I was the only person who stood by you. I don't even know the whole story, but I've always believed something happened to you that night. Please, I'm begging you. We couldn't figure it out when we were kids, but I think I'm on to something now."

Jaime closed her eyes and struggled to hold back the tears that were threatening to fall. She could feel her hands shaking badly, and her heartbeat picking up its pace. Something had happened to her fifteen years ago, and the entire town thought she was crazy or making up stories, except Flynn. He was the only person who truly believed she had experienced something awful that night. Her own parents had thought she was on drugs when they first got to the police station, and then when that proved false, they just thought she had misinterpreted what she had seen.

"It was just your fucking imagination, Jaime. You're always watching that horror shit. It was only a matter of time before you scared yourself half to death."

Fifteen years later, and those words still rung through her head like a bell. That night was one of the reasons she hadn't been home in seven years, and why she always insisted that her parents travelled to Maine for holidays. That night was why she would wake up sometimes in the middle of the night, screaming, clawing at her clothes trying to get free of that stupid bush. That night was why she didn't go near the woods anymore. The girl who grew up camping and hiking couldn't even take a walk in the woods without getting lightheaded. What she would give for all of that to finally end. The nightmares and panic attacks and feelings of helplessness. She was tired of being afraid, and tired of running away.

"Okay," she said so softly Flynn had to lean in close to hear her words. "Let's do it."

Flynn let out a breath he didn't he even he was holding.

"There's my girl," he said cracking a smile.

"So, you think you finally got a handle on what this thing is?" Jaime asked standing up to refill their mugs.

"Fifteen years is the key." Flynn said opening the shoulder bag he had brought with him. Inside were piles of folders, each filled with pages and pages of newspaper clippings and photocopies from books. "When the first story appeared in March of someone disappearing from town, I started digging again. There hadn't been a missing person's report for fifteen years in Hawk Ridge. At first, I thought it might be just a coincidence. I didn't want to get my hopes up, but as I got deeper into everything, I realized it was a pattern."

Here Flynn opened up a folder and pulled out several missing person's reports.

"Here look," he said spreading the yellowing papers out in front of them both. "2002. Carrie Stevens went missing in April. Mark Roberts was next in July. Terrence Julip was the last in August of that year. Those ones we already know about."

Jaime nodded, remembering their time as junior investigators as kids.

"Then, 1987, the year before we were born. Three more names of missing people throughout that year. 1972, three more names. 1957, that year I found five names of people who had simply disappeared. The only two things that all of these people had in common, was that they were last seen in Hawk Ridge, PA and that they were never seen again. I went all the way back to when the town was founded in 1811, and every fifteen years, it's like fucking clockwork. There are several disappearances throughout each of those years."

"So what is it that's taking these people? You make any headway on that since the last time we searched?" Jaime asked flipping through the stack of missing person's reports. There were faces of 'men and women', 'black and white', 'young and old', and everything in between. Whatever was hunting and taking people didn't have a type, it liked everything and anything it could get its hands on.

"I still have no idea," Flynn admitted. "There are stories from basically every culture around the world about creatures that kidnap or eat humans. It could be anything. I have a working theory though."

At this, Jaime looked up from the table.

"This thing shows up every fifteen years. It takes anywhere from three to ten people, from what I've uncovered. Why does it take more people some years than others?"

Jaime tilted her head to the side, trying to think of a reason for such discrepancy, but couldn't. She shook her head indicating Flynn should continue.

"I don't know. It's hungrier some years than others?"

"Exactly!"

When Jaime furrowed her brow in confusion, he continued. "I think this thing is taking sacrifices. Think about it, the town was founded in 1811 and for that year, I found records of six people going missing, but who knows what the numbers actually were. It's not like the records from back then were rock solid. I think someone, a founding member of the town, made a deal with something. A deal where every fifteen years, that thing would come back and take as many people as it believed it needed in order to protect the town and its people for another fifteen years."

"Okay," Jaime said nodding her head. "I can get behind that. But why does the number of sacrifices vary from year to year? Isn't something like that usually pretty steady when it comes to legends like this?"

"I have a theory on that too. I think that if this "protector" knows it's going to a hard fifteen years, nationally or just in Pennsylvania, it needs more lives. Check this out," Flynn said flipping through another folder looking for a certain document.

"1929. The Great Depression rocks the entire country, but this article written for the *Hawk Herald* in 1935 claims that our town shouldered on throughout the Depression with very little hardships. Look at this line, 'It would seem that Hawk Ridge has a guardian angel watching out for it during this extremely difficult time.' But get this, 1927, just two years prior to the start of the Great Depression, eleven people went missing that year. That's the highest number I've found so far for any year."

Jaime read the entire article, carefully swallowing each word. Everything Flynn was saying made sense. Someone, somewhere in their little, blue collar, all American town was offering their friends and neighbors up as sacrificial lambs. It reminded her of that short story they had read in high school English, Shirley Jackson's *The Lottery.* Jaime had loved it when she had first read it, had thought it was chilling and great storytelling, and she had loved the dark twist. Now thinking about it she wanted to be sick. Thinking of that story, however, made her think of something else. If the townspeople in Jackson's fictional town knew about the ritual, and still took part in it every year, then couldn't that mean the citizens of Hawk Ridge, or at least some of them, knew about this fifteen-year cycle?

"Do, uh, do you think people know what's happening?" Jaime pondered, pushing the news article across the table where she wouldn't have to look at it anymore. "That there are people who just let this happen every fifteen years?"

"I think it's a solid possibility. There are a ton of people who are direct descendants of the founding members of Hawk Ridge. I really wouldn't be surprised if this secret has been passed down from generation to generation. I would be willing to bet that this person, this entire family, thinks of themselves as protectors, a family of knights. They've probably rationalized it in their heads that they're doing this for the good of the town. They see another missing person's report pop up in the *Herald*, and they think, this is the way it must be. This is the way it's always been. As for the whole town knowing, that I can't be sure of, but I doubt it."

Silence filled the small kitchen. Jaime sat there drinking in everything Flynn had told her. The morning sun filtering through the kitchen window bathed them in a warm light. Despite this, and the warm coffee mug clutched between her hands, Jaime felt a chill rise up her spine. Flynn sat next to her hoping that she would still agree to come home with him. He needed a second pair of eyes with this, and she was the only person he trusted. He couldn't do this without her.

Several minutes passed, and still the two best friends sat in silence. Finally, Flynn asked Jaime the question that he had been dying to ask for fifteen years.

"Jaime," he began slowly not wanting to startle her. "What happened that night to you?"

Jaime flared her nostrils and clenched her fists. Flynn hoped that he didn't just ruin everything, but he needed to know. If they were going to do this together, they needed everything out in the open.

"You know what happened. The whole town knows what happened," Jaime gritted out between clenched teeth.

"No," Flynn responded gently. "No, I don't. I know you saw something in the woods that night that scared you to death. I know your parents, Amber's parents, and a lot of the police made it seem like you imagined something, or that you made it up. But I never thought that. I always believed something happened to you that night. I never asked you about it before because I didn't want you to push me away."

Jaime opened her mouth to counter, but he cut her off before she could get a word in.

"Jaime, I know you. Had I pushed the subject, you would have closed yourself off, pushed me away to 'protect' me from what you had experienced or some bullshit. I kept quiet because you had already lost Amber, I didn't want you to lose me too. But now I need to know the truth. I need to know what I'm, what we're getting into with this. Please, Jai."

Jaime closed her eyes once again, and then quickly opened them, afraid of what she might see in her closed eyelids.

"Okay, but you have to wait till I finish to ask any questions. Otherwise, I may not get it all out.

When he nodded and swore he'd let her get all the way through her story, she took a deep breath and then started talking.

"You know the first part, that part was always true. That was the only part a lot of people ever really cared about."

Four

October 2002 – Pennsylvania

"It's getting late. I really need to get going before my parents stumble into my room and realize that I'm not there." Jaime whispered to the other occupant of the bed she was currently residing in. Despite her words of departure, she made no attempt to move.

A small sigh escaped from beneath the mass of chestnut colored curls on her chest.

"I know. I just – I don't want you to go."

Jaime let out a sigh of her own, and then placed a firm kiss on top of the curls. She inhaled deeply, and was assaulted by the smell of cherries and vanilla, which was quickly becoming her favorite shampoo scent. Then, fighting against every urge inside of her, she began to untangle herself from Amber.

"I know. I'm sorry. I wish things could be different. Maybe in a few years they can be. Maybe we can find a college where we can just be ourselves, and not have to worry about your parents bursting through the door at any moment, and then dowsing us with holy water."

Jaime was trying her best to make Amber laugh, but what she got was just a sad smile. They both were now trying desperately not to cry. Despite the joke they both knew if Amber's parents ever caught them together there would be worse consequences than holy water. On a similar night to this one Jaime had flat out asked Amber what would happen if her mom stumbled upon them. Amber answered that she didn't know for sure, but that there would be lots of yelling. They both laughed at this, but then Amber grew serious.

"I'm not exactly sure what it means," she began. "But I saw her reading an article about conversion therapy a few months back on the computer. When she realized I was in the room, she nearly fell out of the chair trying to close the window. I haven't had the guts to look it up yet."

"Hey," Jamie cooed sitting back down on the bed. She grabbed Amber's right hand in her left, and laced their fingers together. "I promise one day it's going to all work out. We just have to be smart until that day comes."

Amber tried to smile again, and was a little more successful this time.

Before she could talk herself out of it, Jaime leaned in and pressed her own chapped lips to Amber's. Amber's chapstick was the same as her shampoo, and Jaime suddenly felt lightheaded. After several seconds she forced herself to pull away. She really did need to get home. Now when Amber smiled, it lit up her entire face.

"I'll see you tomorrow." Jaime felt her own face form into a smile. She grabbed her backpack and then crossed the room to the lone window in Amber's room. She slid the window open easily and climbed out onto the roof that overhung the porch. She eased herself down as close to the edge as humanly possible. It was only about seven feet from the bottom of the roof to the ground, but Jaime still needed to be careful. One misstep and she could easily twist an ankle or worse, and then their cover would most definitely be blown. She sat with her feet and legs dangling over the side of the roof. Carefully, she eased off her backpack and tossed it to the ground a few feet away from where she planned on landing herself. Before she could overthink anything, Jaime simultaneously used her arms to push her off the roof and flung her legs out as if she was jumping off a moving swing. She quietly landed a few feet away with the grace one only possesses at fourteen. She grabbed her backpack off the ground and then turned around to shoot a thumbs up to the shadow in the window from which she had just escaped. When she got one in return, Jaime turned to make her way home where if everything went as planned her parents would never know she was out until almost midnight.

During the day, the town of Hawk Ridge resembled something out of a storybook. Neat little homes lined the streets, kids played in perfectly manicured lawns, flags supported the high school football team hung from almost every porch, and neighbors waved to each other while they collected the mail. At night, however, Hawk Ridge became something out of a horror movie, at least in Jaime's mind it did. The entire town was nestled in a valley surrounded by towering pine trees and sprawling fields. The quickest way from Amber's house to Jaime's was to cut through one of these fields, which ran about a half a mile, and then through a stretch of about a hundred yards of woods. Once through the woods, it was only about another five hundred yards to Jaime's front door. Jaime could take the long way home, but out on the streets she was more likely to have someone peek out their window and see her trotting down the sidewalk. It wouldn't take long for the phone to ring in Jaime's house, and her parents to discover their daughter was not nestled asleep in her bed.

Jaime had grown up playing in these woods and fields, and yet at night, she couldn't help but feel a shiver make its way up her spine. The farmer who owned this particular field had already taken in the corn that had grown here for the year, so Jaime was completely exposed as she hustled through the rows of leftover stalks. Somewhere between a fast walk and a jog, Jaime had watched enough horror movies to know not to take her time making her way through a corn field at night. The incessant crunching of dried husks beneath her feet set her on edge more than usual, and she felt herself grinding her teeth against the noise. She didn't think there were any houses close enough to hear the crunching, but she still couldn't help but feel paranoid.

About three-quarters through the field, her feet ceased to move. Her instincts were suddenly telling her to stay still, don't move a muscle. *You're just being paranoid,* she told herself. But she couldn't shake the feeling that she was being watched. She tilted her head and strained her ears, listening for any indication she was being followed. She could have sworn she had her distant crunching other than her own. After a few agonizing seconds, she spun around sure she would see nothing, succeeding only in freaking herself out more. It was October. There were leaves all over this godforsaken town. Even a small breeze could send some flying and produce that crunching sound. Her eyes darted from side to side, searching the trees on that side of the field for something she knew she wouldn't find.

"Shit!" She exclaimed as her eyes landed on something she wasn't expecting to see. Out in the open field her voice sounded foreign to her own ears. The trees seemed to throw it right back at her, making it echo in her head. After a second her heartbeat returned to normal. Antlers. It was just a fucking deer lingering back in the trees. Another non-surprise for the middle of October in Pennsylvania. Jaime, herself, didn't hunt, but she knew a good majority of the town did, and come deer season every year most of them were able to bag themselves a new prize.

She turned back around to continue her way home and made it about seven steps before she paused again. Her heartbeat began to quicken once more. Her body was telling her to just run the rest of the way home, to get the fuck out of there, NOW. But she forced herself to turn around again. This time her surprise caught in her throat and Jaime would swear to her dying day that she physically felt her heart slam to a stop in her chest for a second.

The deer was closer now, maybe only five or six feet from where it stood thirty seconds ago, *why didn't the leaves crunch,* but it was now out of the cover of trees illuminated by the near full moon. And it definitely wasn't a fucking deer. Deer didn't stand or walk on their back legs. Nor did they wear black robes.

Jaime had learned all about adrenaline last year in biology, and how when the body sensed danger it either went into fight or flight mode. What her teacher didn't tell her about adrenaline was the agonizing few seconds of utter helplessness the body went through before one of those decisions kicked it.

    Jaime stood unmoving for what felt like several minutes, but what was in reality about six seconds before her flight mode beat out her fight mode. Finally, she tore herself out of her stupor, and bolted for cover in the nearby trees. It hadn't rained in well over a week and the ground was hard and dry for which Jaime was thankful. She entered the tree line and beat down the path that had been carved out after years of foot traffic through this set of woods. Suddenly, her foot caught on a root hidden by the night and she was sent sprawling and landed in a small bush. Her chin clipped the ground and her teeth clacked together painfully. Her hands clawed at the dirt as her feet tried to find steady ground. Against her better judgment, she glanced behind herself. It was closer now, much closer. In the open field, Jaime was probably a good seventy-five to hundred yards away from this thing. Jaime had always been one of the fastest sprinters in her grade, boy or girl, and she thought she had had a decent head start. But whatever this thing was, it didn't move like a human or a deer, for that matter. It didn't as much as walk as it did glide. Her eyes kept being drawn back to the antlers, and she didn't want it to get close enough so that she could see what kind of face was hidden under the hood of the robe.

As quick as she had fallen, she was back up again legs pumping and lungs burning as if they were filled with battery acid. She could see the streetlights through the edge of the trees, and knew she was almost home. Home. Shit. No way was she going to take this creature to her front door where her parents were sleeping.

New plan Jaime, you need a new plan she roared at herself. *Come on! Think!*

She didn't need to turn around to know that the thing was gaining ground. She had watched enough horror movies to know that it would be a fatal mistake to take the time to turn around now. She needed all her focus on where she was going. Then it hit her. The police station was just down the street. If she could just make it there, even if she made it close enough for them to hear her screams when this thing got its hands on her, *did it even have hands?* she might have a fighting chance. Now with a plan, Jaime found her second wind and sprinted for the police station.

As she ran, Jaime lost all concept of time. After what seemed like hours, she barreled through the front doors of the police station and threw herself at the front desk. The cop who was sitting there jumped up, and nearly pulled his firearm when Jaime came sprawling through the doors and landed on the floor gasping for air. The shock on his face was immediately replaced with concern when he realized there was a teenage girl flopping like a fish on his floor.

"I need some help out here!" The cop roared as he came rushing around the desk to see what was going on.

Three more cops soon appeared in Jaime's line of sight. One she recognized as Flynn's Uncle Danny. The others she was sure she knew, but at the moment she would have been lucky to get her own name right.

"Jaime!" Flynn's uncle called to her. "Hey! Jaime what's going on?"

Her breath was coming in short, painful gasps. Her chest felt like it was full of fire, and she was beginning to see spots. Another cop lifted a bottle of water to her lips, and she drank greedily.

"You're okay, sweetheart. You're okay," Uncle Danny said. "Let's get this backpack off of you."

She didn't really remember it, but she assumed they lifted her up enough to slip the straps off of her arms and lay her down flat on her back.

"Something," she managed to gasp out. "Something behind me."

Uncle Danny jumped up with his hand on the butt of his gun.

"Lewis, with me,"

He disappeared with the guy who had been sitting at the desk through the front doors to see if they could find what had scared this girl so badly. Moments later, they reappeared saying they couldn't find anybody. At this point they had managed to get Jaime up and sitting in a chair. She was trying to finish the bottle of water, but her hands were shaking so violently and she was still breathing so heavily, that she ended up spilling a lot of it down the front of her sweatshirt.

"Jaime," Uncle Danny began as he crouched down in front of her. "What the hell happened? Do your parents know where you are?"

She was finally starting to come back down from her adrenaline high, but she still jumped at the sound of his voice. After another minute of catching her breath and collecting her thoughts, and she began to speak.

"No one is ever going to believe me. None of you are going to believe me. Holy shit. I don't even believe me."

She was still out of it enough to not hear Uncle Danny turn to one of the other cops and tell them to call her parents. Had she heard him say that, she would have fought tooth and nail for them not to. They were going to give her hell. She hadn't even thought about Amber and her parents at this point yet.

An hour later, Jaime was still sitting in the station chair. Her breath had come back, but she couldn't stop shaking. Someone had draped a blanket around her shoulders, but she had a feeling the shakes had nothing to do with the air conditioning in the station. Her parents had arrived about ten minutes after they had been called. They were furious and scared out of their minds. Her mom was crying off and on, and she could tell her dad was struggling to keep it together. Fuck. This was bad. Worse even than that time she had fallen out of the tree at her friend Jenny's house and everyone had been worried she might have had a concussion.

Once her parents had arrived, Uncle Danny asked Jaime to tell them all what happened from the beginning. Don't leave anything out, he said, no matter how crazy it sounds, his eyes finished. So Jaime told them. She told them where she had been for most of the night. She told them she had climbed out of a second story window and monkeyed her way off of the roof. She told them that she was nearly home free after another secret rendezvous with the girl who she was hoping to make her girlfriend one day. She told them how she had initially spotted the antlers in the trees, and how the deer had nearly given her a heart attack. She told them that when she realized it wasn't a deer, she thought she was going to be one of those people who disappear and are never heard from again. She told them that she couldn't explain what this thing was, but she knew deep down in her heart that this thing was playing with her. She told them that she believed the only reason she made it through the front doors of the police station was because this thing had allowed her to. She finished her story, then grabbed the trashcan next to the desk she was sitting at and vomited.

Everyone within earshot fell into a dazed silence as Jaime retched up her dinner. They all managed to wait until she had finished, and had control again before everyone seemed to react at once.

"Why did you feel the need to hide the fact you were gay from us?" Her mom cried, tears pouring from her eyes. "Did you really think we wouldn't love you anymore!?"

Her sobs shook her entire body, and somehow Jaime felt even worse now than she had two minutes ago. She hated seeing her mom cry, even more when she was the reason her mom was crying in the first place.

"If you are under the influence of anything right now, young lady, you won't be leaving the house again until you're eighteen."

Her dad was furious, she could tell. His face had grown bright red, and Jaime could see his clenched fists shaking. What she didn't know was that he was shaking in fear more so than rage. When he had first picked up the house phone to discover the police were calling about Jaime, he was terrified they were going to ask him to come identify her body.

A sudden bark of laughter escaped from Lewis' lips, and Jaime flinched at the sound. Not that she hadn't been expecting it. She was surprised everyone wasn't laughing at her by now. He was quickly quieted by Uncle Danny turning on him and telling him to go take care of something else in the other room.

The other cops all stood looking at each other, wondering if they needed to administer a breathalyzer or drug test. Uncle Danny was the only one to really address her as an adult during the whole situation, something Jaime never forgot.

"Jaime," be began. "What did this thing look like? You said it had antlers. Are you sure it wasn't just a deer?"

Jaime tried to remember something, anything, but couldn't. She shook her head.

"No." she squeaked out. "It was really dark. The body was covered in a big, black robe looking thing, like the fucking Grim Reaper or something. The antlers are the only thing I really remember. I think I was trying not to look at its face."

"Okay. I'm going to take your parents into the other room for a minute, alright?"

She nodded instead of speaking, afraid that she might burst into sobs at any second.

Uncle Danny and her parents were gone for a long time, or at least it felt like it. When she glanced over at the wall clock behind the desk she was surprised to see it had only been about ten minutes since they had gone into the other room. The clock, itself seemed to mock her. It was an ordinary wall clock, but instead of numbers on each hour, there were animals native to Pennsylvania. She glanced at each animal seeing how many she could identify to pass the time, when her eyes fell on the animal where the number six should have been. The state animal of Pennsylvania, the white-tailed deer. This one stood on a hill, overlooking a valley that only it could see. On its head sat a rack of at least ten points. Jaime sat transfixed on this picture, imagining what would have happened if those antlers had caught up with her on that night. The image on her being gorged and lifted off the ground swam into her head before she could push it away. She felt her stomach flip again, and forced herself to turn away from the clock.

Finally, before she could have any more visions, Uncle Danny came back out alone. He walked back over to her and crouched down so that they were eye to eye. Jaime had always liked Flynn's Uncle Danny, she had always liked Flynn's entire family.

He was quiet for a minute. She kept her eyes focused on her hands in her lap. She discovered she had been picking at her fingers without even realizing it, and her left thumb was oozing blood. *So much for kicking that bad habit.* She thought before lacing her hands together to stop herself from causing any more damage.

"I'm not sure what it was you saw out there tonight. I do know that it scared the hell out of you. Your parents are worried about you. They seem to think you're on some kind of hallucinogenic drug."

Jaime opened her mouth to protest, the idea of her doing drugs was ridiculous, but was cut off by Uncle Danny continuing.

"I don't think you are."

At this, Jaime clamped her mouth shut again a little surprised someone believed her.

"Your parents are worried that since you were keeping you and Amber a secret, that you've been keeping other secrets, hence the drugs. I've seen a lot of people on drugs over the years. From marijuana to heroin to crack cocaine and everything in between. I told them that that's not what this is. I told them that you probably saw a monster buck and that in the shadows cast by the moon. Your imagination then turned it into something it wasn't."

Jaime thought again about protesting, but bit her tongue and remained quiet.

"I know that's not what happened, but I think your parents are okay with that version of the story. I don't know what you saw out there tonight, Jaime. I have no idea what scared you so bad that you felt you had to run here instead of running home. Just promise me no more sneaking out at night, okay?"

Jaime nodded and bit her tongue even harder to keep the tears pooling in her eyes from spilling over on her cheeks.

A minute later her parents reappeared to take her home. Her mom's eyes were red, but thankfully the tears had stopped. Jaime could tell they were still irate with her, so she thought it was best to keep quiet unless she was spoken to. The drive home only lasted about two minutes, but it was long enough for her parents to ground her for a month and to make her promise she wouldn't keep any more secrets.

"School and then home, nowhere else until Thanksgiving. Are we clear?"

Her mom's voice was a bit stronger now. The fear wearing off, and more anger taking over.

"Yes ma'am."

Jaime was in no mood to bring up after school clubs and activities, and she had a feeling neither did they.

"It was just your fucking imagination, Jaime. You're always watching that horror shit. It was only a matter of time before you scared yourself half to death." Her dad's voice seemed to echo in her head even now, years later. "How the hell do you confuse a deer for a fucking monster?"

Instead of responding, Jaime remained silent, biting her cheek to keep the tears pooling in her eyes from leaking down her cheeks.

It was well after 2 A.M. when they arrived home and Jaime finally got to bed. She didn't expect to sleep, but once her head hit her pillow she had a surprisingly dreamless night of sleep. By the time she woke up the next day it was almost noon and she realized her parents had thankfully let her stay home from school for the day. She rolled over and reached for her cell phone on her bedside table. Her mom would be on lunch soon and she wanted to send her a text thanking her for letting her sleep. What she found when she looked at her phone, however, was twelve messages from kids from school. Somehow, everyone seemed to know what happened the previous night, including Amber. Most of the texts read something like,

'R u crazy!?' and 'Don't let the monsters under the bed get you!'.

She had one from Flynn asking if she was okay and if there was anything he could do.

Of all of the messages, good and bad, Amber's text of simply 'my parents know', was the only one to twist her stomach into painful knots.

Five

"You pretty much know the rest," Jaime sighed sipping the last bit of coffee in her mug. "That afternoon once school was out, I called you in tears."

Flynn had gone white listening to Jaime recount her nightmare. His hands shook as he ran them through his hair, and then down his face. Now he nodded, himself remembering.

"I brought you ice cream to cheer you up, and then we sat and watched cartoons for hours. Fuck Jaime. I mean I knew about you and Amber, obviously before that night."

Jaime couldn't help herself and laughed at this.

"I knew something bad happened to you that night. I remember your face that afternoon when I showed up. You were haunted by something, something I don't think I would have understood back then. But to hear the whole story, after all these years, I can't believe you held that in all this time."

Jaime shrugged and tried to play it off like it wasn't a huge deal.

"You were the only person, besides your uncle, who actually believed that I wasn't completely out of my mind after that happened. I guess I didn't want to tell you the whole story and have you question my sanity."

"No wonder you were gone as soon as you graduated college," Flynn said sheepishly. "For the longest time, I was kind of mad at you for leaving, and for never coming back to visit. Now, I can't really blame you."

"You're probably the only person in that town who is going to be happy to have me back for a visit besides my parents."

"So you still want to come back with me? You'll help me put an end to this?"

Jaime was silent, and Flynn was sure she was going to say that she changed her mind, that she didn't want to go back and relive that night any more than she already has.

"Yeah," she said finally. "I'm not too thrilled about it, but there are families out there who have no idea what happened to their loved ones. We can't bring back the missing, but maybe we can make it so that no other family has to live without knowing."

The room fell silent for a few moments. Both just content to sit with one another without having to fill the void with talk. Flynn got up to refill their coffee mugs one more time, and then pulled out a new folder from his bag.

"So what else do you have in that magical mystery bag of yours?" Jaime asked after taking a long sip out of her Maine lobster mug. "Anything that might help us figure out where to start with this?"

"Actually," Flynn said a little sneakily, "It just might. I've been doing a lot of research this year. Most of my free time not at work has been spent at the library. In addition to all the disappearances I've looked into, I've also found a few eyewitness reports."

"Other people have seen this thing too?" Jaime asked with a hint of excitement in her voice. If there were other people who saw the same thing that she had, then there was proof that she hadn't made up her story fifteen years ago.

"I was only able to find three other people who reported seeing something strange in or around Hawk Ridge. You make four. But those are the only documented ones I found. Imagine how many people may have seen something, but were too afraid to come forward, or thought they were hallucinating."

Jaime nodded in agreement. She definitely knew what that felt like.

"So these witnesses – tell me what you know about them."

Flynn pulled out the first piece of paper from his new folder and placed it down in front of Jaime. It was a photocopy of an old police report. A very old police report, by the date on the top of the page.

"In 1882 two brothers, thirteen-year-old Mick and ten-year-old Jack McManus, spotted something they reported as being a 'cross between a deer and a bear' by the river on the east side of town. They were hoping to do some fishing on a Saturday morning when they came out of the trees to see this thing darting up the other side of the riverbank. It freaked them out enough that they ran home and forgot all about fishing that day. When they told their parents about the incident, they decided to make a report of it with the police in case there was a sick wild animal in the woods that might wander into town. The police didn't really think much of it, thought it was just some kids who saw a deer covered in mud or something."

"Or they just made the story up," Jaime finished.

Flynn nodded, pulled out a second piece of paper, and continued.

"Flash forward to 1957. Twenty-one-year-old Gary Kinkaid was driving down Laurel Street around sunset when he saw something 'black with giant antlers' standing in the middle of the street about ten yards in front of his truck. Startled him so bad that swerved and nearly hit a telephone pole. Article in the *Herald* says that it caused a little bit of a raucous, some people came running out of their houses when they heard the tires squeal. The police were summoned and they took down his report, but it turns out Kincaid was a little heavy on the bottle, and a lot of people surmised that he had just had one too many that afternoon at the bar."

"I'm starting to see a pattern here," Jaime said raising an eyebrow. "So how does any of this help us?"

"Kincaid's still alive. And he still lives in the area. I called him a few months ago."

Jaime perked up hearing this. Here was someone who could possibly prove her story wasn't a load of shit.

"He didn't want anything to do with me. Said he had put that story behind him, that he was busy, and never wanted to speak of it again."

Jaime's heart fell hearing this. So much for that lead.

"I called him again last night on my way up here. I told him about the latest disappearance and that I was on my way to get someone else who had seen what he had seen. It took a little convincing on my part, but he's agreed to meet with us when you come home."

"You were pretty confident that I'd come home with you," Jaime teased.

Flynn's face turned a little pink, and he ran his hand through his shaggy hair once more.

"I mean, I was hopeful that I could talk you into coming back and helping me. But, I also really wanted to meet with this guy so I kind of had to promise him something that may or may not have been true. He said to give him a call when we were both back in town."

Jaime chuckled and then the room fell into another comfortable silence. Suddenly, Jaime's head snapped up and her eyes widened ever so slightly as a thought popped into Jaime's head.

"What are people making of Amber's disappearance? What do they think happened?"

Immediately Flynn rolled his eyes so hard Jaime thought they would disappear inside his head, and let out an irritated groan.

"People are pretty upset. I think I've heard every theory imaginable on why and how she disappeared. I've heard talk that her parents think she might have run off in order to go back to her 'young sinful behavior.'"

"For fuck's sake," Jaime cried.

"Oh, yeah. Some people are sure a drifter came into town and swiped her up so that they could force her into the sex trafficking trade. No one believes she would ever willingly abandon her family and friends."

"What about Jared? What has he been saying through all of this?"

"He's been playing the role of the distraught husband pretty well. Well enough to fool just about everyone in town." Flynn said between clenched teeth.

"But not you?"

He paused before answering, letting his jaw unclench.

"No, not me. Something's just way off with the way he's been handling all of this."

"And you're sure there isn't any bias coming through with this accusation?"

"It's no secret I can't stand the guy. I've tried to be civil with him all these years, I never wanted to exacerbate anything, but the guy's always been a snake in the grass. He's only ever looked out for himself. Even after him and

Amber got together he always cared more about himself than he ever did for her."

Flynn wasn't wrong about Jared, and Jaime knew it. They had all graduated high school together, and Jaime remembered fairly well how much of a dick Jared always was. The day she returned to school after the chase through the woods was a prime example.

"You're thinking Jared knows about the creature, aren't you? You think one of his family members is the one who made the deal all those years ago, and now he sacrificed his own wife to it."

"It's crossed my mind." Flynn shrugged. "I haven't done a ton of research on what families were here when the town was founded, but I'm sure it won't be hard to find a list in the library or historical society."

Jaime nodded. "When do you want to get on the road? I'm assuming you want to get back as soon as we can."

"We can head out tomorrow morning. As much as I want to get back, I think I need a couple hours sleep before I do that drive again." As if to drive this point home, Flynn gave a yawn that reminded Jaime of a lion from a nature documentary she had flipped through the other night. Suddenly Flynn's eyes flew open wide as a thought came to him.

"Jaime, what are you going to tell your boss? Do you even have the time to take off?"

"I guess I'll say there's a family emergency or something. She doesn't need to know the details. I just handed in my most recent project this week, so it's not like I have any deadlines coming up anyway. And as for time, I think I've taken a grand total of three days off in the seven years I've been up here.

My boss will probably be thrilled I'm taking some time for myself."

Six

The next day, Jaime and Flynn set off on the nearly eight-hour drive from Southern Maine to Northeast Central Pennsylvania in their respective vehicles. They discussed taking Flynn's Jeep and Jaime flying back to Maine once everything was taken care of, but Jaime didn't like the idea of being trapped in her hometown. She promised Flynn that they would see this through to the end, but she also wanted an escape plan just in case. She hoped she wouldn't have to abandon Flynn again. She still felt awful about leaving him seven years ago, but she was a planner, and she liked to keep all of her options open.

They had just popped into a rest stop just over the Massachusetts state line on I-95 to fill up their tanks when Jaime figured it was as good a time as ever to ring up her boss.

"Hey, Martha. It's Jaime," she said when her boss picked up after two rings. "I know it's Sunday, and you're probably busy, but I needed to talk for a second."

"Of course, what's up kid?" The sound of water breaking on rock could be heard in the background and Jaime knew she was sitting out on her back deck drinking her morning coffee. Martha and her husband of twenty-five years, Lon, lived on the coast of Maine overlooking the Atlantic. It had a backyard that seemed to stretch on for miles dotted with apple trees that were picked every fall. Jaime had been over several times for parties and for Sunday brunch. They didn't have any children of their own, but they did have three Portuguese water dogs, Dusty, Papi, and Mookie. Jaime loved their house, and once while there celebrating a coworker's birthday, she had jokingly asked Martha if they could leave her the house in their will. They both had a good laugh about it, but Jaime never did notice the glint in Martha's eyes or the sly smile on her face.

"I need to take some time off. Something's happened back home and I'm headed back there now. I apologize for springing this on your last minute like this, but I didn't even find out about it until yesterday morning." Jaime blurted all of this out at once, afraid if she stopped for even a second she would never get the words out.

"How much time do you need, kid?" Martha asked, concern evident in her voice. Martha and Jaime had clicked from the moment Jaime sat down for her interview seven years ago. Martha had made a joke about Jaime's alleged accent, and quick on her feet, Jaime responded with her own jab about Martha's. The pair had become fast friends despite Martha being Jaime's boss. Martha loved everyone on her staff at *The Way Life Should Be,* but she considered Jaime the daughter she never had.

"Well," Jaime began, her free hand now twisting the braid that hung down from her head. "I'm not really sure. A week at least, maybe more. I'm sorry I can't give you more solid details."

"Kid, you take all the time you need. I know this can't be easy for you, going home and all, so don't you worry about us up here." Martha's 'here' came out sounding 'he-ah'. "We'll be fine until you get back. Send me a text when you get there (the-ah), so I know you made it safe."

Jaime blew out a breath that she hadn't realized she had been holding, and sent out a silent thank you to the heavens above.

"Will do, thank you Martha. I owe you big time."

"Kid, you've already paid me back double these past seven years (ye-ahs). You be safe, I'll see you soon."

About two and a half hours later the pair had pulled over at a diner affectionately named, 'Mabel's Diner,' in a Connecticut town neither of them knew at the moment for a brief lunch stop. The floor inside was black and white checkerboard, the booths were upholstered in red and white vinyl, and a group of old men sat at the counter reading the paper and talking about the weather. The walls were decked out in décor featuring Coca-Cola, John Deere, Chevrolet, Ford, and various other Americana staples. Each booth was equipped with a tiny jukebox ready to play hits from the 50s and 60s. There was even a sign that read *'Please, No Dancing on Tables.'*

Their waitress, Carole, a plump woman in her fifties who kept calling Flynn 'sugar,' had just set down their lunch and they began to dig in.

"So other than Amber disappearing, anything else weird going on in Hawk Ridge?"

"Nothing more than usual really," Flynn said in between bites of his bacon cheeseburger. Jaime hadn't seen this guy in person in seven years, and he was still eating the same garbage he always had, but looked like he could lift a car with one hand. She surmised that working in and around the construction business since you were fourteen would do that to someone. "A lot of the folks we graduated with are still around. A bunch have married each other and are now either pregnant or have several kids under the age of four running around. Most of them still couldn't tell you the proper use of your vs. you're."

Jaime let out a bark of laughter at this, and nearly choked on a piece of her buffalo chicken salad. Then she got quiet and contemplative.

"You ever think about leaving yourself?" She asked Flynn, not knowing if she wanted to hear his answer or not.

Flynn was quiet for a few moments, thoroughly chewing his burger before swallowing.

"Yeah, I do. I've been thinking about it a lot lately. I mean it's still home and all, but it hasn't felt like home for a while now, you know?"

The raised eyebrow let Flynn know that yes, she knew exactly how that felt.

"Sorry, you know better than anyone, I guess. I could probably sell the house easily and make some money doing so. Mom and Dad basically gave it to me anyway."

"Would they be mad if you sold it? You guys have been in that house for as long as I can remember."

Carole had just brought the check and before Jaime could even react to it, Flynn had plucked it from the edge of the table and pulled out his wallet.

"Hey, no. I'll pay for my lunch." Jaime argued.

"Uh-uh. No way. Just because you have a fancy job now doesn't mean I don't get to treat my best friend to lunch. I haven't been able to do this for seven long years. Do you know how many bad dates I've had to pay for during that time? We're going to need to do this several times in order to make up for all of them."

"Ha!" Jaime exclaimed as the two made their way to the counter to pay. "This I've got to hear."

"Later tonight, once we get to my house and get you settled in. We can crack a couple cold ones and I'll tell you all about the dating woes of yours truly."

"I'm going to hold you to that you know." Jaime called as they both climbed into their cars and got back on the road.

It was almost four o'clock that afternoon when Jaime pulled into the familiar driveway. She had told Flynn on their pit stop there was somewhere she needed to stop first before making it over to his house.

"They know you're coming home?" he had asked delicately.

"I called them yesterday after you crashed in the bedroom for your nap. I didn't want any surprises."

"And what did they say?"

"They're ecstatic. They've been up to Maine several times over the years, but they're happy I've finally decided to come home for a visit."

"So what exactly did you tell them? I'm assuming they asked if you had heard about Amber." Flynn inquired.

"I told them she was one of the reasons why I was coming home. I said you had called and told me what happened and wanted me to come home for the vigil."

"How did you know there was going to be a vigil? I never said anything about that."

"Please. I know that town. Wife of the former high school quarterback goes missing in a small town, and you don't think there'll be a candlelight vigil at some point?" Jaime accompanied this remark with an award winning eyeroll of her own.

"So you want to go? It's tomorrow night."

"Not really, but yeah, kind of."

"Whatever you want to do, we can do." Flynn nodded, understanding her confliction regarding the vigil. "We'll talk more about it later."

Jaime grabbed her backpack from the passenger seat and then exited the car. She stared at the front door for longer than necessary before making her way up the gray pavers that lined the front yard to the door. Before she even made it the entire way across the yard, the front door flew open and her mother appeared, smiling from ear to ear.

The older woman's shoulder length, dark blonde hair swirled around her face as she hurried to meet Jaime. Her green eyes shone with unshed tears, thrilled to have her only daughter back home again. In her late fifties,

Cheryl Strait knew she wasn't getting any younger, and knew how special it was to have Jaime back in Hawk Ridge. When the two women met on the front porch, Jaime was immediately crushed against the smaller woman's 5'3" frame and held there for a solid minute.

"It's so good to have you home, sweetie." Her mother cooed in her ear before finally letting her go.

"Good to be home, mom" Jaime replied, albeit it wasn't exactly the truth.

"How long are you staying?" her mother asked as she shuffled her into the house.

"Not sure yet," Jaime said twirling the end of her braid between the fingers of her left hand. It was her tic as well and she knew it, but sometimes she still couldn't help it. "A couple days, maybe longer. I was hoping to maybe help with Amber's search."

"Terrible thing, what's happened." Jaime's mother lamented. "No one seems to have any idea where she's disappeared to. Come on, let's go see your father."

Jaime didn't even need to guess where her dad was currently. She may have been gone for seven years, but some things never change. Her mom led her out on the back deck and there he was, riding his John Deere riding mower around the backyard. Her dad always complained how much he hated mowing the lawn, but somehow he always seemed to be doing it. He had just turned the mower back towards the house, and a few seconds later he spotted his wife and daughter standing on the deck. He smiled and waved, his short, brown, thinning hair wafted in the slight breeze as he drove the mower over their way. Between both parents, Jaime most definitely looked more like her mother. However, her and her dad shared their baby blue eyes. Jaime met him down at the bottom of the stairs, and could see tears pooling in his. A second later she was once again crushed for a few seconds. He smelled like freshly cut grass and gasoline, and Jaime actually found herself having to hold back tears of her own. Some things never change.

Seven

February 2003 – Pennsylvania

The snow had been falling nonstop for almost twenty-four hours. The Hawk Ridge School District was closed for the second day in a row, and most of the town was also shut down. The milk and bread had been cleaned off every grocery store shelf in a ten-mile radius, and the residents of Hawk Ridge were preparing for several more days of waiting out the storm.

Flynn was seated at his kitchen table eating a bowl of Fruity Pebbles when he heard the tell-tale three raps at the front door. Not even bothering to swallow his current mouthful, he jumped up and swung open the door to reveal his best friend banging her boots off on the front porch, and shaking the snow out of her fuzzy, red, beanie.

"Come on in before all the heat gets let out," he attempted to say around his mouthful of cereal.

"Dude," Jaime laughed, hurrying into the warmth. "No wonder you don't have a girlfriend." She reached up with her hat and wiped away the milk that had dribbled down onto his chin.

"The only reason I don't have a girlfriend, is because you don't approve of anyone from this town," he countered after he finished chewing.

Jaime shot him a look of mock disbelief as if to say, *who me*? At this they both broke into laughter.

"You want some breakfast before we head downstairs?" Flynn asked when the laughter died down.

"Nah," she said shaking her head. "Mom made me eat before I walked over."

"We've got plenty for lunch when you're hungry again," he responded, waiting for her to kick off her boots and strip out of her bulky coat.

Once she was rid of her outerwear, she followed Flynn over to the basement door, and down the stairs into the Baygo wreck room. Several years back, Mr. Baygo had converted the basement into a room where Flynn could take his friends to play videogames, watch movies, and just hang out. It was an immediate hit with Flynn and his friends. The latest addition to the room was the old computer from Flynn's dad's work office. He, himself, had just upgraded his computer system at work, and decided to set up the old one in the basement.

"The internet might be a little slow with all the snow, but it still should work okay for what we want." Flynn said as he pressed the power button on the tower. The room filled with a sound similar to a small aircraft taking off, as the computer comparable to a dinosaur warmed itself up.

Jaime nodded, pulling up a chair to sit next to Flynn at the small desk. The two of them sat hunched over staring the monitor waiting for the Window's 98 screen to finish loading. Once finished, Flynn double clicked on the Internet Explorer icon, and waited for the little hourglass to disappear. Several, painfully slow moments later, the home screen loaded, and a search bar appeared. Flynn moved his hands into position above the keys, paused, and then turned to face Jaime.

"What exactly am I looking for?"

Jaime furrowed her brow, and scrunched up her face, in an effort to help her brain produce the right words.

"I'm uh, not sure. I'm the one who saw it, and I still don't know what to freakin' call the damn thing. I know what people are saying, but it definitely was not an animal. I wouldn't be here if it was. That thing let me live."

"This is going to sound crazy," Flynn offered. "But what if we just did a general monster search? Whatever chased you obviously isn't Dracula or Frankenstein's monster, but there are cultures all over the world who have their own boogeyman."

Jaime mulled this idea over for a second. Suddenly, she remembered a TV special she had watched one Friday night when her parents were out somewhere. It detailed an old Native American folklore legend, the wendigo, a cannibalistic monster. There were several interviews with people who had told their alleged encounter with the beast. Jaime remembered wondering that night, what could scare someone so terribly, that they'd claim they saw a monster? Now, after everything she had been through, she knew exactly what those men and women had experienced.

"It might be crazy," she replied. "But crazy's all we got right now."

The next two hours were spent sifting through internet searches on monsters. They were no closer to identifying what it was Jaime encountered now than they had been when they first began. Jaime was beginning to become increasingly frustrated knowing that there was something out there, but no one else seemed to know it was there.

"Why hasn't anyone else from town seen this guy?" Flynn wondered aloud, moving the mouse to click out of another webpage. "This is a town smack dab in the middle of the woods. Most people spend their every free moment running around in the woods. So, either this thing has the greatest hiding spot ever."

"Or it was just a deer that chased me." Jaime said with a sound of resignation in her voice.

"Or," Flynn continued ignoring Jaime's doubts in herself. "It has the ability to not be found."

"So, a ghost? You think I was chased by a ghost?"

"There are spirit legends from all over the world. The list of people who claim they've been visited by spirits goes on and on. It could be a possibility."

"Okay, let's just dial up the Ghostbusters then," Jaime joked.

The look of hurt that briefly crossed Flynn's face told Jaime she'd gone a little too far. She sighed and then leaned forward until her forehead rested against the desk.

"I'm sorry," came the muffled words. "You're only trying to help, and I'm being a jackass. Truth is, the more I think about it, the more I begin to believe that I was just tired and I hallucinated, and there wasn't anything there with me in that field that night. I'm not sure which option scares me more."

Flynn placed a comforting hand in the middle of her back, and began to draw circles over her hooded sweatshirt.

"Why don't you go over to the couch and flip the TV on? Find something mindless to watch for a while, and I'll keep digging over here."

"I don't deserve your friendship," Jaime replied as she stood up and moved over to the overstuffed couch.

"You say something like that again, I'm taking you outside and throwing you in a snowbank."

Jaime let out a hearty laugh, one that she needed, and then turned the TV to a movie and let herself get lost in a cheesy, straight to VHS, action movie from the 80s. She had no clue what the title was, but she didn't care. Flynn would let her know if he found anything of merit, but for right now, watching bad special effects and over the top fight scenes sounded better than reading blogs about wendigos and werewolves.

An hour later the credits were rolling. The good guys had defeated the bad guys and had saved a South American village, and soon, a new movie was getting ready to start. Jaime felt her stomach rumble, and decided it was time for a snack run to the kitchen. She was just about to ask Flynn if he wanted anything while she went upstairs, when he let out an exclamation from his spot in front of the computer.

"Son of a bitch!"

"You got something?" Jaime rushed over to see what was on the outdated computer screen.

Her eyes glanced over the monitor, and she prepared herself to come face to face with the monster again, but there was no monster. On the screen she saw a news article. Flynn wasn't even looking at a monster website anymore. Instead, he had pulled up the online version of the *Hawk Herald* and was reading through some articles.

"You mean there was something in the *Herald* about this thing?" Jaime wondered, now full on confused.

Flynn remained silent, and continued to read, silently mouthing the words as he went.

Finally, when he finished the current article on screen, he popped open one of the other tabs on the browser.

"What do you see here?"

Jaime looked at the title of the article at the top of the webpage, and skimmed the first couple of lines.

"It's a story about a missing person. Looks like Carrie Stevens went missing April of last year. No clue who she is."

"Now what about this one," Flynn continued as he opened a new tab. Up popped an article featuring a picture of a man in his thirties kneeling on the ground dressed in hunting attire. In front of him sat a turkey that probably ended up as Thanksgiving dinner that year.

"Another missing person, Mark Roberts, from–" her eyes searched the text. "–July of last year. Both from Hawk Ridge?"

Now on a roll, Flynn opened one more tab.

"And last, but not least."

"Another one from August of last year. Terrence Julip. Hey, I remember that one. He was the older guy who used to come to all the high school's sporting events, right? Principal Hart even gave him that letterman jacket with his name on it one year. What the hell happened to him?"

"Nobody seems to know. This article is from the day after he disappeared. It theorized he got confused and wandered off into the woods. They coordinated a search party and everything for him. There's another article from about a month and a half later, urging people who thought they knew something to contact the police. A lot of people in town really loved this guy."

"So, why did you show me these?" Jaime prodded, still a little confused.

"Have you ever heard of any other people disappearing from this town? Or even people who've gone missing for a brief period of time?"

Jaime thought about it for a second, and then had to admit that she hadn't. Her dad watched the six o'clock news every night after supper, and she couldn't think of any other nights where the top story was someone who had simply disappeared. Three disappearances in one calendar year in one town as small as Hawk Ridge was a bit strange.

"Right. I even went back six or seven years, as far back as I could find, and I couldn't find any other disappearances. I know this could be a leap," Flynn explained. "But what if this monster is connected to these missing people somehow?"

"As in? It took them?"

Flynn shrugged his shoulders and scrunched up his face to show he wasn't positive, and that it was a working theory.

"Okay, I can get behind that. But now what? If nobody believed me when I said that I saw a monster, they sure as hell aren't going to believe that monster is responsible for the disappearances of those people last year."

"There's nothing we can do to help prove our theory except to wait for more people to go missing."

Eight

Dinner at the Strait residence that night consisted of hamburgers and hotdogs on the grill. The three of them sat out on the deck under the September sunshine enjoying their family meal catching one another up on current events.

"You're liking your job?" Her mom asked as she spooned some potato salad onto her own plate. "And your boss? She's treating you well?"

Jaime nodded with enthusiasm as she finished her mouthful of hamburger.

"Martha's great. She's always having the staff over to her house for brunch and parties. You'd die if you saw their backyard, mom. Right over the ocean."

"How's the apartment? Everything good with the heat for the winter? Weather Channel says it's going to be colder than normal for the entire northeast this winter." Her dad asked as he squirted some ketchup on his second hot dog.

"The landlord had someone cleaning the furnace just the other weekend, so I'm sure it's good to go."

Jaime reached across the table and grabbed another handful of BBQ chips and a second hamburger. *This is actually really nice.* She thought as her mom brought out three more bottles of Yuengling for them.

"What's new around here?" Jaime asked as she popped the top of her beer. "Besides the obvious, any other major news?"

It was as if Cheryl Strait had been waiting all night for this question, because she immediately began rambling about the latest controversies of Hawk Ridge.

"Amy Cormier is pregnant again. Can you believe that? Three kids all under four. At least they're all with the same guy, unlike that girl you used to play basketball with. What was her name?"

At first Jaime wanted to make a comment that there were several girls who fit this description who she had played basketball with, but she knew exactly who her mom was talking about.

"Kim Hart."

"Ugh," Harry Strait chimed in. "I never liked her. Could never learn how to guard the pick and roll, that girl."

"That and she would spend more time talking to boys at the away games than actually playing basketball." Jaime added. "How many kids does she have now?"

"Four!" Cheryl exclaimed. "With three different men!"

"Homecoming Queen, my ass." Jaime muttered into her beer.

"Oh! Joey Daubins has been arrested again. He was high on bath salts making death threats against an ex-girlfriend of his. Police had to use their tasers on him and everything!"

"Kid was a hell of a Little Leaguer and football player, but pretty shitty at being a decent guy."

Jaime nodded in agreement with her father. Joey was one of the guys who used to run with Jared in high school, and had probably dated most of the girls in their graduating class. She wasn't sorry at all to see him behind bars again.

The question and answer portion of the night went on for another hour and a half until

Jaime delicately mentioned she needed to get going over to Flynn's. Her parents knew that she was going to be sleeping at Flynn's while she was in town, which was only one street over, but they still hugged her tight and made her promise to stop back in tomorrow when she left for the night. Her dad suggested they could all go get ice cream or something.

It was about seven o'clock when she rolled into Flynn's driveway, still exactly as she remembered it. The sun was starting to fade, but they still had some decent daylight left for the day, and neither of them wanted to waste it.

"So how'd it go?" Flynn asked as he met her in the driveway to help her carry her things inside.

"They've already made me promise to stop by tomorrow," Jaime replied slinging her backpack onto her shoulders. "I also got the entire rundown of who's engaged, in jail, and pregnant. You have to promise me you won't ever get together with someone from high school. I don't think I could take it."

"Don't worry. No plans in that department anytime soon. Come on, let's get your stuff inside, and then we're going to go for a ride."

"You going to give me the official welcome back tour of town?" Jaime joked tossing her backpack on one of the chairs at the kitchen table.

"Something like that," Flynn smirked.

Not long after the pair was sitting at a table outside of their favorite place to go growing up. The Karnish Creamery had the absolute best hand-dipped ice cream around, and Flynn and Jaime had spent many a night in high school hanging out at these tables. The two had inhaled their ice cream cones (chocolate marshmallow for Flynn, mint chocolate chip for

Jaime), and were now reminiscing about times long gone.

"I still think that night Bobby McFlaine ate four large cones in a half hour is one of the best nights we had in high school." Flynn said leaning back in his lawn chair, letting his ice cream digest.

"That kid could eat anything," Jaime added in. "I think I about peed myself watching him get that brain freeze afterwards. I for sure thought his face would stay that way, with his eyes all scrunched up willing it to go away. Whatever happened to him?"

"I think he lives over in Crawford now. Married a girl from over there, still looks like he could eat just about anything."

"So what's the next stop on this welcome home tour?" Jaime queried. So far, she was actually having a good time being home.

"Well," Flynn began. "I thought we could take a drive by the football field, since that is where Amber was last seen. Maybe we can find something that might help us in identifying whatever this thing is."

Jaime had to admit she wasn't crazy about the idea, but she knew coming into this that she was probably going to have to go places and even talk to people she would rather leave in the past.

"Let's do it, while we still have some light left."

Another short drive later and the pair found themselves at their old high school. It looked exactly the same as it had when they were in high school. Built in the late 40s, the outside of the building remained about the same since its construction. Inside had been updated over the years. Overall, it was a very well-kept building. Three stories of classrooms stood over the school grounds. A few of those classrooms located in the back of the building on the third floor offered perfect views out onto the soccer and baseball fields. The school was home to about four hundred students and about fifty-five teachers, who shared parking spots in the main lot in front of the building. Jaime and Flynn parked in one of the smaller lots on the west side of the school, located near the football field.

There were decorations plastered all over the fence surrounding the field, and Jaime guessed inside the school was even more decorated. Everywhere she looked there were signs reading, 'HAWK PRIDE' 'YOU'RE IN HAWK COUNTRY' and 'FEAR THE HAWKS'. Along with the signs were hundreds of red ribbons tied to the fence spelling out 'HAWKS' in giant block letters. It was something she remembered the cheerleaders doing while they were in high school. The football team here hadn't had a winning season since 2013, but you could always count on the school and town being pumped up for the first game of the season. Everyone always believed that this was the year they would turn the program around.

The gates to the field were swung open and they could see plenty of people from town utilizing the all-weather track; some walking, and some jogging. Jaime and Flynn passed through the gates and under the sign that had welcomed home and away teams and visitors to the field for as long as anyone could remember, 'WELCOME TO THE NEST.'

"From what I hear, Amber left her seat sometime in the third quarter to go to the restroom, and then never came back. Jared's one of the coaches now, so he didn't even realize she was missing until the end of the game. The vigil tomorrow is going to be held here. People have been setting up a kind of shrine in Amber's honor, so I guess they figured this was as good a place as any."

No sooner had Flynn got the words out of his mouth did Jaime spot the shrine. At least people had the decency to do it under the scoreboard and not directly outside the bathroom, Jaime thought. Flowers were laid everywhere, Jaime counted at least two dozen bouquets of all types of flowers. There were also several pictures of Amber, one with her husband, one with her parents, and even one from high school.

"Nobody knew that her favorite flowers were daisies?" Jaime asked almost angrily. Flynn placed a gentle hand on her shoulder.

"Come on. Let's have a look around." Flynn said as he led her away from the scene and over towards the restrooms.

Not wanting to draw attention to themselves, the pair leaned up against the cement block building that served as the bathrooms for the football field. They casually glanced around as they tried to spot anything that looked out of the ordinary – anything that might have indicated Amber put up a fight, or tried to leave a trail. They stood with their backs pressed against the hard wall for nearly fifteen minutes, but they came up with nothing. Nothing looked like it had been disturbed, no paint chippings that indicated someone tried to grab onto the wall, no blood. Nothing.

"I pretty much expected this, but thought we should give it a look over anyway." Flynn looked defeated. "Come on. Let's get back to the house and I'll tell you about those bad dates."

This got Jaime to crack a smile for the first time since walking out onto the track and seeing the shrine. Just as they were nearly back to the gate, however, they heard a voice from the past that made them stop cold.

Nine

October 2002 – Hawk Ridge High School

The idea of returning to school after everyone had found out what happened to her filled Jaime with pure dread. Her stomach felt like it was full of cement. She hadn't been able to eat anything for breakfast that morning, and she doubted she'd be able to eat lunch that afternoon. Jaime was at least thankful that Flynn still wanted to be her friend after hearing the abridged version of what had happened the previous afternoon.

The duo made their way up the walkway to the front doors of Hawk Ridge High School. To Jaime, the walk seemed to last forever and end too quickly at the same time. Her stomach might have been empty, but it still felt like she was going to vomit at any second. She imagined the other students, her friends, lined up on both sides of the hallways waiting for her to walk through the doors so they could laugh at her. The girl who cried monster, they'd probably call her. She pictured kids running around her with their arms raised above their heads making wooing sounds like a pack of ghosts, and then laughing their heads off when she flinched. And then on top of all of that, there was Amber.

The text message reading 'my parents know' still stung Jaime's eyes. Every time she closed them, she could see the words blazing on the back of her eyelids. She had responded to Amber when she had first seen the text.

"How much do they know?" She asked. "How did they even find out?"

"Enough," came the response. "This town keeps secrets as well as a sieve holds water."

A few seconds passed and then another message came through.

"I heard about what happened after you left my house last night. Everyone at school has heard. I'm guessing one of those shithead cops told someone, who told someone else, and well, we all know how that goes."

"Awesome," Jaime typed. "So, what happens with us now?"

"I'm basically on lockdown. I'm not allowed to go anywhere except school and youth group at the church on Wednesday nights. Mom will probably ask for me to be cleansed or something. They also say I can't spend any time with you outside school."

On any other day, this would've gotten a laugh out of Jaime. Amber's parents were devout Catholics, and her and Amber were always joking about what they'd do if they found out their daughter was gay. But now that it was actually happening, it just made Jaime want to cry.

They went on texting for a little while longer until Amber said her parents were going to be home from work soon, and that she had to delete these messages so they wouldn't see them. They both promised the other that they'd figure a way to work things out, and that they'd talk in school the next day.

Back at the school, Flynn pulled open the front door and held it for Jaime to walk through first as usual. Jaime held her breath for the onslaught she was sure would come, positive the upperclassmen would torture her and her fellow freshmen would disown her. She came to a stop in the front hallway of the school wanting to see who she would have to face first, but it was empty. She let out the breath she was holding and thanked a god she still wasn't sure she believed in. Flynn came up beside her and nudged her with his elbow.

"Come on," he said gently. "I'm right here."

The front hallway was a small lobby of sorts. It connected to two longer hallways that ran parallel to each other. They were filled with the classrooms and students' lockers. Those two went on to join up with a third hallway, the longest of them all, filled with more classrooms and lockers. Flynn and Jaime's lockers were in one of the two parallel hallways with the other freshmen and some seniors. *Here* Jaime thought, *here is where it'll start.*

They turned the corner and laid their eyes on about thirty or so students getting their books ready for the day, or congregating amongst friends waiting for the first bell. With a gentle hand on her elbow, Flynn led her down the hall to their lockers. They passed little groups of students and some heads turned around to see who was coming down the hall. A few snickers could be heard from a group of senior girls as the pair passed them, and a freshman boy nudged his friend who was busy on his cell phone to show him who was walking by, but that was the extent of the torture that Jaime was dreading.

She relaxed a little as she arrived at her locker and began spinning the lock's combination. Right 32 – Left 23 – Right 3. Click. She opened the door and was nearly buried under a mountain of something. A sound of surprise escaped her lips, and she could now hear the laughter of pretty much everyone around her. Once the shock wore off she realized what had nearly smothered her. Hundreds of pieces of paper. A second later she realized what was on those papers. Deer. Pages ripped out of magazines, images printed out from the internet, even some hand drawn pictures on notebook paper. Every single one of them had some kind of deer picture on it. Jaime felt like passing out, but she knew that would just draw more laughs. She pushed away the blackness that clouded her vision, and then felt Flynn's hands on her upper arms steadying her for good.

It was then that the apparent ringleader of the operation stepped forward through the rest of the students.

"We all got together and decided we wanted to help you identify what a deer looks like. That way you don't have to go running to the police next time you see one in real life."

The voice was recognizable immediately. Jared McCloskey. The soon to be star of the varsity football team. Jaime had known him her entire life, and had never been a fan of his. He was the quintessential jock/bully.

He had always picked on kids half his size or those younger than him throughout middle school and soon to be high school. But because he was the football star, he was able to get away with a lot more than other kids could. One time in seventh grade during gym class, he had drilled another boy in the head with a dodgeball so hard, it made his ear bleed. The ball slipped he claimed, and because no one could prove otherwise the game went on as if nothing happened. Jared's antics always seemed to be swept under the rug.

"How retarded do you have to be to think a deer is some kind of monster?" Jared cried which was met with more laughter. "They need to put you in the Sped classes, dyke. You and the other retards can color deer pictures and drool all over each other."

"Enough!" Flynn bellowed turning away from Jaime and towards Jared.

Normally Jaime would've been pissed with Flynn for fighting her battles for her, but today she was really glad that he stepped in. Jared was way too much of a pussy to mess with someone like Flynn. He preferred his victims small and helpless, and Flynn was neither. Although usually mild tempered, Flynn stood at a staggering 6'1" as a freshman. By the time they graduated, he would top out at 6'4". No other male in their graduating class would even break 6'0".

Smart enough to know when to stop before he got the shit beat out of him, Jared grabbed his backpack and set off to his first class of the day.

"See you later, deer girl!" He cried turning the corner of the hall. His laugh could be heard for several more seconds after he disappeared.

It didn't take long for everyone else to realize that the show was over, and they dispersed a moment later as well.

Flynn turned back to his best friend once the last of the stragglers had disappeared to see tears forming in her eyes.

"Can't wait to go through four more years of this shit," Jaime tried to joke. "And thank you. I don't deserve a friend like you."

"Hey," Flynn chided softly. "Don't let me catch you saying something like that again, or no more ice cream and cartoon nights."

When Jaime laughed Flynn smiled knowing that for the moment he had accomplished his mission. He knew however, the battle was not over, not by a long shot. When someone like Jared found something that got under someone's skin, he gripped it tight and held on for the long haul.

Ten

August 2017 – Hawk Ridge High School "The Nest"

"Well, shit!" Jared McCloskey exclaimed. "Never thought I'd see the day Jaime Strait came back to this neck of the woods."

Jaime and Flynn turned to face their classmate. He still looked pretty much the same as he had in high school. His short sandy blonde hair was ruffled slightly by the bit of wind that had picked up. He still looked like he worked out regularly, although he appeared to be about fifteen pounds heavier than his "glory days" in high school. He wore khaki pants and a red polo. On the left breast was his name JARED sewn in gold thread with the words QUARTERBACK COACH underneath. *Of course, he's the quarterback coach,* thought Jaime. *Asshole always thought he was going to be the next Dan Marino. When that didn't pan out as he planned, because he sucked total ass, he probably figured the next best thing would be to coach the next Marino.*

"Figured I'd come pay my respects." Jaime responded. She was trying to keep the anger and disgust out of her voice. "I'm sorry about Amber."

At the mention of his wife's name, Jared's eyes darted away from hers for just a second. He recovered quick, frowned, wiped his eye, and said his thanks, but Jaime knew she hadn't imagined what she had seen. This asshole knew something.

"The vigil is going to be tomorrow night at seven right here at the field. Father Collins is going to say some words."

"He's still alive?" Jaime found herself asking. At least she was making an attempt at being civil, even when it reality all she wanted to do was knock his teeth in. "Wasn't he in his seventies when we were kids?"

Jared actually chuckled at this, and Jaime found herself second guessing what she had seen in his face a few seconds ago.

"He's been retired from the church for a couple years, and he uses a cane now, but Amber's family and I thought it would be nice if he spoke. He married us, you know."

No, Jaime thought. She didn't know. Amber's parents had drilled it into her head that she was sinning and she needed to find a 'nice boy' with whom to settle down with. Once she had found out that Amber was seeing Jared, the prick who had tortured her in high school, she cut the last remaining ties with her. Sure, she tried to be happy for her, but she could never really get over that feeling of abandonment. She never even got an invitation to the wedding.

"Well, we'll be here tomorrow," Flynn spoke up after a few awkward seconds of silence.

"See you then." Jared said turning away to go back to wherever he had come from.

The duo walked in companionable silence back to Flynn's Jeep. Once they were seated with the doors shut they turned to one another simultaneously.

"Please tell me you saw that," Jaime asked.

"He knows something." Flynn answered with the same excitement in his voice. "I knew it. He's got the whole town fooled. Who would ever suspect the former football star turned coach?"

"So now what?" Jaime asked. "Where do we go from here? He'll never let us in their house to poke around."

"We have to go speak with Gary Kinkaid," Flynn countered. "We have to see what kind of information he might have up his sleeve."

Jaime nodded. She didn't want to get her hopes up, but it was looking like they were finding more and more pieces to the puzzle.

"Tomorrow morning you can ring him up, see when he wants to meet with us," Jaime said as Flynn turned the key in the ignition. "But right now, I want a beer and to hear about those dates of yours."

The next morning, Jaime sat at Flynn's kitchen table drinking a cup of steaming coffee. She could hear Flynn on the back porch finishing up his phone conversation.

"Great. Thank you, we'll see you then," Flynn said while opening and closing the back door, joining Jaime at the table.

"So? What'd he say?" Jaime inquired.

"We're going to meet him at his home this afternoon around one," Flynn said, fixing himself his own cup of coffee. "He still sounds a little apprehensive, but I think when he sees that we're legitimate, he'll feel a little more at ease."

Jaime nodded. "Good. So that gives us plenty of time to head to my parents' house for a few hours."

Hearing this, Flynn paused with his mug halfway to his mouth and a look of confusion plastered on his face.

"I promised my parents that I'd stop by today. I haven't been home in seven years. I cannot break that promise, or I'll never hear the end of it. Mom asked about you last night too. She would love to see you."

"Fair enough. Give me twenty to shower and we can head that way now. It might be a little difficult finding Gary's house, so I want to give us plenty of time to get lost and still get there by one. He doesn't seem like the type of person who likes being left waiting."

Once Jaime heard the shower turn on, she began to reminisce. She had spent a lot of time in this house growing up. A lot of math homework had been done on this very kitchen table while Flynn's mom had made them hot chocolate or lemonade. There were a lot of good memories in this house for Jaime, but the one that kept coming back to her was the night she told Flynn she was moving to Maine.

She was home for Easter break from college, and it was the Saturday night before Easter. Her and Flynn had spent most of the day playing basketball in his driveway. Once it had started to get dark, they made their way indoors to the living room. Jaime couldn't remember what they had on the television, but she remembered she was drinking blue Gatorade and Flynn had orange. For all the similar interests the two shared, Gatorade flavors were not one. Flynn's mom kept a special stash of blue in one of the cupboards just for her. Jaime had been dreading telling Flynn that she had gotten the job in Maine and was going to be moving all day, but she knew that sooner or later he would find out, and she wanted it to be from her.

"So you know how I went to Maine for that interview a couple weeks ago?" Jaime asked, trying to be nonchalant.

"Yeah," Flynn said in between sips of Gatorade. "You get any lob-stah while you were there?" He added the New England accent on purpose, trying to be funny.

"They offered me the job on the spot." she blurted out. Not exactly how she had wanted this to go, but Jaime didn't want to drag this out any longer. "I'll be moving after graduation in May, and my first day will be the first of June."

Flynn didn't respond right away, and Jaime's heart broke. Finally, after what seemed like forever, he spoke.

"I knew they'd hire you!" He exclaimed jumping up off the couch and pulling her up into one of his bone-crushing hugs. "I'm so proud of you!"

"Thanks Flynn," she breathed out relieved. "You think your dad will give you some time off down the road to come visit?"

Flynn had worked for his dad's contracting company since he turned fourteen. He loved working construction, and he loved working with his dad, but he still didn't know if he wanted to take over the business one day.

"I think I might be able to work something out with him," he laughed. "But seriously, congratulations. I'm glad you're getting out of this town. You're made for much bigger things."

Flynn said all the things Jaime had been hoping to hear that night, but she still couldn't help but feel guilty. She knew that deep down he was probably upset that she was leaving, but he hid it well. She hated the idea of leaving him in this town while she moved on. She desperately wished she could have taken him with her, but she knew at that point in time his dad would've blown his lid if Flynn would've mentioned leaving the business.

They did a pretty good job of keeping in contact for the last seven years. They followed each other on all the usual social media, texted constantly, and phone calls were made about once a month. They even video chatted a few times when they both could be in front of their computers. But it wasn't the same as being together in person. Jaime couldn't help but think of how long they would have went without seeing each other if Flynn hadn't jumped in his Jeep and came and got her. She felt a little sick thinking about it.

Suddenly, she was jarred from her thoughts by Flynn coming back into the kitchen.

"You good?" Flynn asked. He had seen her jump when he came back into the room.

"Just lost in thought. I have a lot of fond memories of this house."

Flynn smiled in return.

"Hey," she said, suddenly remembering something. "You never answered me about if your parents would be mad if you sold the place."

Flynn shrugged and ran a hand through his wet hair. Uh-oh, Jaime thought.

"They probably wouldn't be too happy at first, but I think they'd eventually come around. I've been seriously considering it for about a year now. I could get a job in construction pretty much anywhere."

"Kind of like journalism," Jaime added with a smile.

"Yeah," he nodded. "Maybe once everything is taken care of here, I can think things through a little more thoroughly. I don't want to rush into anything."

A comfortable silence fell over the kitchen, and the two best friends sat drinking coffee with no need to say anything to fill the quiet. An hour or so later, they grabbed their backpacks and drove the thirty seconds to Jaime's house.

The rest of the morning was spent with Jaime's parents, who were thrilled to see Flynn once again. They bombarded him with questions about how his dad's business was going and if he was going to take it over one day.

"Mom!" Jaime exclaimed after her mom questioned whether or not he had finally found himself a girlfriend. "I didn't bring him over here so you could interrogate him."

"It's okay, Jaime," Flynn chuckled. "Some dates here and there, but nothing permanent. It's hard to find a girlfriend when your dad is grooming you to take over the family business one day."

Jaime's mom clicked her tongue in disapproval, but nodded her head in understanding.

"Don't you let him work you too hard," she scolded. "You've always been a hard worker, you deserve to enjoy your life."

Around noon, Flynn shot Jaime a look that said they needed to get going so they would get to Gary Kinkaid's house on time. The pair managed to leave without much of a fight, but not before they were made to promise to stop by again as soon as they could.

    Kinkaid lived just outside of Hawk Ridge in an area that locals simply called The Valley. It was an area inhabited by mostly farmers, dairy cows, goats, and even a bison farm sprinkled the fields. A lot of the kids who grew up in The Valley went to school in Hawk Ridge, so Jaime and Flynn knew their way around the area fairly well, but there were a lot of back roads and small dirt paths that could easily get someone turned around and lost for a bit. It was down one of these roads that Kinkaid had built his small cabin. It was only by a stroke of luck that Jaime spotted the unmarked dirt road as they almost blew by it. A lone black mailbox with the numbers 657 hand painted in white on the side identified it as the road Kinkaid had relayed to Flynn as his driveway.

The driveway twisted and turned for nearly a mile through thick Pennsylvania woods. The trees grew close together back here, and the branches of ancient looking oak trees loomed over the road blocking out the sun. Jaime was glad they had brought Flynn's Jeep because the several watermelon sized holes that they had to negotiate by going off trail. Flynn didn't dare go above fifteen MPH. He was afraid he might hit a hidden hole and blow a tire. This was not the place he wanted to get stuck near or after dark.

Just when Jaime thought she'd die of anticipation, the road opened up, the sun shone through the trees, and Kinkaid's cabin appeared in front of them. The structure sat nestled underneath a pine tree that had to have been close to a hundred feet tall. The shadows from the tree painted the cabin in a spooky, *Scooby-Doo* type of light. The porch, which ran the entire length of the front of the cabin, appeared to tilt dangerously to one side. A lone window sat dark, and unwelcoming just to the right of the front door. An old Ford pickup truck that looked like it had once been blue but had faded to more of a gray sat just to the right of the front porch. Jaime guessed that this guy didn't leave his house all that often besides to go for some groceries every couple of weeks. She looked at Flynn behind the wheel and raised her eyebrows. She was really hoping that this guy wasn't some Ed Gein type or something. Flynn pulled the Jeep around the small driveway and pointed the front end towards the way they had come in, just in case he told himself. He shot Jaime one last look, grabbed his bag out of the back seat, and opened his door.

The front porch creaked under their weight as Flynn knocked on the front door, which swung open almost immediately. Gary Kinkaid looked to be in surprisingly good health despite being in his eighties. His hair had gone gray, his teeth looked to be permanently stained with coffee and tobacco, and he walked with a bit of a limp, but he still looked like he could hold his own if need be. He invited them in and showed them to his living room which also doubled as the kitchen. There was clutter everywhere, but it was a tidy clutter. Everything had its own little place. Jaime and Flynn sat down on the couch that he'd clearly had since the seventies judging by the brown and green plaid pattern that covered it. Kinkaid plopped himself down in the recliner opposite them, that he'd probably had for just as long. Between them was a wooden coffee table littered with a few Busch beer cans and old junk mail.

"I'd offer you folks a drink, but I have the feeling you're itching to get down to business here," Kinkaid spoke up for the first time. "But before you say anything, I need the both of you to listen up."

The soft old man face that had answered the door suddenly went hard and stern. He looked at his two guests through eyes that had narrowed to slits. This old man was not fucking around.

"Every single person I have ever told this tale to has either laughed in my face or called me a lying drunk. I stopped telling people about what I saw that night some forty odd years ago. I built this cabin back here away from that town and its people so that I wouldn't have to hear the snickers of children and their parents when they saw me on the street. You have one minute to convince me why I should break the promise I made to myself all those years ago to never tell another soul what happened that night."

Eleven

Jaime knew this was her part of the job. With a deep breath, she opened her mouth and told him her own story. She told this man whom she just met about the worst night of her life. She told him about sneaking out of Amber's house and making her way across the field. She told him of turning around and seeing the antlers for the first time, of turning around the second time, and how she realized that it wasn't a deer that had been watching her from the edge of the trees.

She told him of running, and then falling, and then staggering to her feet and running again. She told him how her lungs burned like they were on fire, and how she was so afraid this thing would follow her home that she instead ran to the police station. She told him of her parents coming to get her at the station – how they thought she was on drugs and how her mother had cried. She told him of going home and falling into a dreamless sleep, and then waking up and reading the messages on her phone. Finally, she tells him of the next day at school and the hundreds of deer pictures pouring out of her locker on top of her.

Once she finished, Jaime sat staring Kinkaid right in the eye. She silently dared him to call her a liar, just like everyone else had, but he didn't. Instead he remained silent for a moment before leaving the room without a word. He disappeared into a room Jaime figured was his bedroom. She looked at Flynn and he just shrugged his shoulders. She could read his thoughts though because she was thinking the same thing, if he comes back out here with a shotgun, we're as good as dead.

When he did return, he wasn't holding a shotgun. Instead, he was holding an old, weathered cardboard box. It was a box one might see police detectives keep evidence in for a murder investigation. He placed it on the coffee table, scattering a few of the Busch cans in the process. He lifted the lid off and placed it down besides the box. He reached inside and pulled out several folders and gave a handful of each to Jaime and Flynn. They flipped open the top cover to reveal the papers inside, and came face to face with things they had seen before.

Jaime examined the newspaper clippings noticing they went back as far as the 1800s. It was all the same stuff that Flynn had dug up, and even some stuff that he hadn't. Certainly, Kinkaid had been conducting research on this thing for a very long time. Among the newspaper clippings and photocopied book pages was a stack of drawings, done by Kinkaid himself. Some of them were done in a very rough and frantic manner, pencil strokes haphazardly crossed the paper in every direction. In some places the pencil had actually ripped through the paper. These Jaime guessed he had done soon after he saw the creature. Jaime imagined how violently his hand must have been shaking as he wanted to get what was in his head down on paper. Over the years, his hands steadied and the drawings got better, clearer. No matter how many times he drew this creature, it never left his memory. He was stuck with it, haunted by it.

"I never thought I would show this box to anybody else while I was still alive," Kinkaid began. "I always figured that once I died someone would stumble upon it, and toss it aside and dismiss them as the hallucinations of a drunk. I always figured it would end up burned in a fire, and this would continue on until the end of time. For sixty years this has been my cross to bear."

With this, he bowed his head and fell silent. For a moment, Jaime thought he had fallen asleep, and then her heart lurched when she thought he actually might have died right there in front of them. When he finally lifted his head, he looked like he might burst into tears at any moment.

"Mr. Kinkaid, sir," Flynn said in his soothing voice. "What happened to you all those years ago?"

Kinkaid blew out a breath and then reached for a glass of water on the table next to where he was sitting. He finished the glass in two big gulps and set it back down with shaking fingers.

"It was November 15, 1957. It was a Friday," he began setting the scene. "All the leaves on the trees had mostly changed and fallen to the ground. There were still a couple stubborn ones hanging on, but the wind had been a nightmare that entire day and by the end of that night they would all be on the ground. I had just clocked out of work at the old Kerry dairy over in Lakeside. I was walking out the door with my good friend Puck Winters discussing plans for the night. I was twenty-one and cocky, it was the weekend, and I was ready to party. My friends and I were planning on painting the town red that night. I just wanted to get home, jump in the shower, and meet my pals at the old Farley Tavern."

"That time of year it's already dark out at quittin' time. Combine that with all the deer around here, and I had to take my time driving home whether I liked it or not. If I destroyed my Ford Ranger on a deer, I'd have to either walk or hitchhike my way to and from the dairy every day, my father had made that crystal clear. And that would have killed my nightlife, so I couldn't have that. I was always tempted to push my luck, especially on Friday nights, especially that night."

Here, Kinkaid paused to get himself another glass of water. Flynn offered to get it for him, and before Kinkaid could decline, Flynn was up off the couch. Flynn was quicker than Kinkaid could have been even sixty years ago, and he returned with three glasses, one for each of them. With a shaking hand, Kinkaid drained half of his immediately. He then pulled a handkerchief from the pocket of his jeans, and wiped the sweat that was forming on his forehead. He paused for a second longer, and then got back to his story.

"The drive from the dairy to my house usually took about twenty minutes, even going slow enough to watch out for deer. But something inside me told me to take it extra slow that night. It was killing me inside. I just wanted to get to drinking, but I listened to that little voice inside my head. I think it probably saved my life that night, and it definitely saved my truck from being destroyed."

"I was almost home. My family's home was on Callahan Street, right down the hill from the railroad tracks. I still hear the whistle in my head when I'm trying to sleep some nights. I was about to make the turn on Callahan from Laurel. Back in those days, there was almost nobody living on Laurel. Mostly was just woods and fields out that way. I was on the homestretch when I saw it. This big black giant about ten yards in front of the truck. It didn't dart out in front of me. It was just there like it had been waiting for me. At first I thought it was a bear, but then I saw the antlers. These giant, hulking antlers. I grew up hunting in this area, and I have never seen antlers that big on a white tailed deer before. It also stood steady on two legs, something I have never seen a deer do, before or since that night. Everything after that moment seemed to happen in slow motion. I've never experienced anything else like it. My mind was in a fog. Nothing was working right inside me. My right foot felt like a cement block by the time I pressed it down on the brake. I felt my hands jerk the steering wheel to the side in shock, but by the time I realized I was doing it, it was too late to correct myself. I heard the tires of the truck screech, but it sounded like it was somewhere in the distance instead of right underneath me. It wasn't until I hit the ditch on the side of the road and the truck came to an abrupt halt that my senses started coming back to me. I sat stunned in my seat for a second, and then spun around to look back to the road. Sure as shit, there it was. Still standing in the middle of the road, still waiting. I don't remember it having a face, just a black hole. I have no idea if I simply blocked it out, or if it simply didn't have a face."

Here Kinkaid paused, once more wiping his face with the handkerchief. Jaime couldn't tell if he was wiping sweat or tears away, perhaps both.

"I don't know how long I sat there staring at it on the road. Might have been a minute, might have been an hour. Time seemed to stand still for me. Then, as abruptly as it was there, it was gone. I watched it disappear into the trees on the other side of the road. It didn't so much as walk away, but glide, or float, or something. It was there, and then it was gone. But I know what I saw that night."

"Not long after it disappeared, must have been a few of minutes, the first couple of folks arrived. They had heard the tires screech and the truck hitting the ditch and came running to see what happened. Police showed up not long after. I told them what I saw, and they all looked at me like I had six heads. First thing anyone did was smell my breath to see if I had been drinking. I insisted I hadn't been. Call the dairy, I cried at them, I had been there all day with the guys there. They all would go on to say that I hadn't had a drop all day, but people still just assumed I had snuck a few drinks at lunchtime, or had stopped somewhere on the way home. Well, you two know how fast word gets around in this town, and it wasn't long before I was the laughing stock of town. After that, I kept my head down, went to work, came home at night, and didn't do much else. Until one day when I got angry. I knew without a doubt that I had seen something that night. So, I started spending my time in the library doing research. Maybe this thing had been spotted before, maybe there was a name for this thing. That was when I stumbled on the disappearances. Every fifteen years like clockwork people in town disappeared without a trace. I checked the papers for the year when I saw this thing, and sure enough, I found records of several disappearances. That's when I knew. This thing, whatever it was, was responsible for all these disappearances."

"So did you ever figure out what this thing is?" Flynn asked with a hint of excitement in his voice. If they knew what it was, they could find a way to kill it, or banish it.

Kinkaid nodded and then reached for a folder that was sitting on the coffee table.

"Over the last sixty years, I have spent a lot of time in the library. I've read probably every book on the paranormal, folklore, and spirituality in there twice. Once computers started coming around, and Mary the librarian helped teach me how to use one, I scoured every website on the occult. I can't be one hundred percent sure, but I believe that this thing is a type of demon." Kinkaid opened the folder, pulling out several sheets of paper. On them were photocopied pages from different books he had found in the library. "Everything I've found points to someone, most likely a founding member of the town, making a pact."

"A pact with the demon?" Jaime asked as she leaned forward to rest her forearms on her knees. She could feel her pulse begin to quicken, and her whole body start to thrum.

"No, not with the demon." Kinkaid placed the papers aside, and looked the pair dead in the eyes. "I believe whoever started this wanted to protect their new town made a deal with Satan himself."

Jaime and Flynn felt their mouths fall open. *Satan?* Jaime thought. *He must think we're gullible idiots.*

"Are you – are you serious?" Flynn asked, echoing Jaime's thoughts.

"More serious than I've ever been about anything. This is something I don't take lightly. There are legends and folklore of people selling their souls to the Devil all over the world. What I think happened is that someone summoned the Devil and offered their soul in exchange for the town's protection. I think what shows up every fifteen years is one of the Devil's demons who comes for collection."

"You have any idea how to stop this thing? How to break the deal?"

"Well, it's not an exact science, but there's got to be an agreement or a contract somewhere. From what I've read about things like this, the original person who summons Satan is the one who signs the contract. Probably with their own blood. That person is long gone by now, but it still comes for payment every fifteen years. My guess is that the contract itself has got power in it, and in order to break the deal you have to destroy the contract."

"That sounds simple enough," Jaime said sarcastically. "Any clue where this contract might be located or who might have it?"

"Over the years, I've made a lot of lists of family names whose ancestors I believed may have been the culprit. All the names on this list were founding members of the town, who have experienced little to no disappearances over the years. I don't have a computer or a television out here, but I still grab a *Hawk Herald* when I go to the grocery store every couple weeks, and always keep an eye out for stories on missing persons in it. I've whittled it down to a handful of names who I think are the most likely. Most of them either have had a lot of success over the years, hold some high positions throughout town, or have just plain been lucky. There's also the possibility that everyone who ever knew about the contract is now dead, and things just keep playing themselves out every fifteen years."

He then pulled out another sheet of paper from his box and handed it over to Jaime.

"You recognize any of the names?"

Jaime skimmed over the names. She recognized a few of them. Hawk Ridge was a small town after all, and then her eyes fell on the last name.

"Holy shit," she exclaimed, as she passed the paper over to Flynn. "Check out the last name on this list."

Flynn grabbed the paper, and his eyes widened immediately.

"McCloskey. That's Jared's family."

"You two know someone with this last name?" Kinkaid asked with a hint of excitement. Having people around who were more connected to the outside world came in handy he was quickly finding out.

"The last person who disappeared this year." Jaime explained. "My friend Amber. Jared McCloskey is her husband. He's actually been at the top of our suspect list from the beginning."

"Well, I'll be damned. You're thinking he got tired of his wife and sent the family demon after her?" Kinkaid gathered. "It would make sense that whoever holds the contract can pick and choose who gets sacrificed if they so desire."

"We have to find and destroy this contract." Flynn said. "Before anybody else disappears this year. And especially before Jared gets wind that we know what's going on and he sends his pet after us."

"Do you have any idea where the contract could be, or how to destroy it? Or what it would even look it?" Jaime asked Kinkaid. "You must have a theory on that at least."

"I've thought long and hard about this over the years," he began. "For a long time, I thought they'd keep it in a safe deposit box. But then I realized that they would probably want easy access to it at all times. That led me to two thoughts; One, a fireproof safe in the family home. Or two, a separate location that couldn't easily be tied to the family, but somewhere that they could still get to it fairly easily."

"What kind of place fits that description?"

"My best guess? The town historical society or the library."

"Hey, yeah!" Flynn jumped in. "How easy would it be to slip something like a contract into a whole building full of other books and papers and important documents?

That would pretty much guarantee its survival all these years."

"No one in their right mind who works at those places would ever just throw something out that they stumbled upon in there." Jaime added. "I would bet that no one's even found it yet. When we had to do our senior research projects in high school, I spent a lot of time in that library. It was always better than the school's, and usually less crowded. One day I asked the librarian, Mrs. Allsbach, a question about a newspaper article or something, and she took me downstairs to their basement. They had so many boxes and filling cabinets down there filled to the brim with things they just don't have room for upstairs, but they never had the time or manpower to go through them to see what is worth keeping and what they could donate to somewhere else. If that's what the library basement looks like, imagine what's down in the historical society's basement."

Kinkaid was lost in thought for a minute and then.

"My bet would be the historical society. Both the library and historical society have been around since the early 1900s, but only the historical society was started by descendants of the founding members of town. Take a look at this."

He pulled out an old newspaper clipping from one of the folders on the table. It was from 1911, one hundred years after the founding of the town, and it depicted the ribbon cutting ceremony of the historical society of Hawk Ridge. Six descendants of some of the founding members of town stood on the front steps of the building. The caption of the photograph read: *Sarah Worth, John Thomas, Michael McCloskey, Ruth Lansky, Jay Wynskeim, and*

Peter Williams, all direct descendants of founding members of Hawk Ridge, Pennsylvania, celebrate the opening of the town's new historical society.

"McCloskey!" Jaime and Flynn exclaimed upon reading the caption.

"Three of those other names are on my list," Kinkaid added. "But I'm starting to think you two are on to something with this McCloskey fellow. As for destroying the contract, I would go with fire. Fire's been known to be a cleansing tool used in many different cultures. Fire is talked about in the Bible over and over, both as a destroyer and a bringer of light. Take for instance, Luke 3:16 which reads 'John answered, saying unto them all, I indeed baptize you with water; but one mightier than I cometh, the latchet of whose shoes I am not worthy to unloose: he shall baptize you with the Holy Ghost and with fire.'

But then in Matthew 25:41 fire takes on a different meaning. 'Then shall he say also unto them on the left hand, Depart from me, ye cursed, into everlasting fire, prepared for the devil and his angels.'"

The room fell into silence once more. The three conspirators each sat in their respective seats shuffling papers through their hands for a moment. Finally, Jaime spoke up addressing Kinkaid.

"Do you ever wonder why it came to you? Why it let you see it without taking you?"

Kinkaid was silent a moment before speaking. "Kid, I've wondered that every damned day since I realized what was going on in this town," he answered solemnly. "There are nights when I sit awake in this chair for hours arguing with myself. Why didn't this thing take me? Why was I the one coming down that road that night? Every fifteen years I think to myself, maybe this will be the year it comes back to finish the job. Maybe, soon I won't have to live with the image of this thing on the back of my eyelids every time I close my eyes. Years ago, I used to think about ending it for myself. One well-placed bullet, and it all stops."

"What made you reconsider?" Flynn asked quietly.

"The idea of this thing still out there, still taking people. That's what kept me going all these years. When I was younger, I was always one step behind it. I could never put all the pieces together correctly. Once I got older though, and figured most everything out, my health kept me from finishing the job. But now that the two of you are here to step into my shoes, hopefully no one else will be forced to live with the burden that we have been forced to live with all these years."

"I guess that means you won't be coming with us?" Jaime asked.

Kinkaid chuckled softly, and then shook his head.

"As much as I would love to, I'm not twenty-one anymore. I wouldn't be very useful."

"Sir, you have been more useful than you know," Flynn said seriously. "Is it alright if we call you if we have any more questions?"

"Of course." he responded. "Please, ring me up at any time. I don't really sleep nowadays, so the hour is not important. I also want you to take my box with you. I think it will be more useful to your battle than it has been to mine."

The pair gathered up all the research spread out over the table, said their goodbyes, and made their way out to Flynn's Jeep. Once buckled in and headed back out on the main road, Jaime turned to Flynn.

"What's our next move? Head to the historical society and tear the place apart?"

"Not yet," Jaime noticed how tight Flynn gripped the wheel. "Let's go to the vigil as planned tonight, play our parts as the grieving friends. We'll keep a close eye on Jared the whole time. If he slips away at any point, and another person goes missing, we'll have even more reason to believe that it's his family's contract."

Twelve

Later that night, as the darkness descended on Hawk Ridge, Jaime and Flynn arrived at the football field for the candlelight vigil. The parking lot was overflowing with cars parked in every spot and along all the sidewalks and lawns. It appeared that just about everyone in Hawk Ridge was going to be at the field tonight paying their respects.

A small stage was set up near the ever growing memorial where Father Collins would soon speak. Jared was standing to the side of the stage with Amber's parents and a few of other football coaches and members of the school faculty. Jaime recognized a few of the teachers and many of the townsfolk who had gathered at the field. Many of the people in turn also recognized her, and immediately wanted to ask her how her life had been going over the last several years. She answered every question politely, and pretended to be interested in what everyone else was doing with their lives, but on the inside, she was dying to get away from these people. Flynn could sense her getting restless and irritated by about the fourth person, so after the cordial but forced conversation, he shuffled him and Jaime away to the edge of the crowd to the left of the stage. They were still able to keep an eye on Jared, but could do so in the shadows of the scoreboard and Jaime didn't feel so bombarded.

"A lot of these people are the same ones who laughed in my face fifteen years ago," Jaime began. Flynn could tell by the way she spoke that she was irritated. "And now they want to know how I'm doing? Nothing ever changes in a small town. Everyone always needs to know everyone else's business." She snapped.

Flynn nodded knowing how Jaime felt and placed an arm around her shoulders.

"We're going to figure this out, and then get the hell out of dodge. I know it's not easy for you to be back here, and I don't want to keep you here any longer than necessary."

"So…" Jaime's voice trailed off as a small smile began to form. "When you say we, you're coming with me?"

"Well, I've been giving it a lot of thought lately, especially these last few days, and –"

Flynn was interrupted by the beginning of the vigil.

"To be continued," Jaime whispered with a grin as everyone turned to the stage.

"Good evening." Father Collins began. The Catholic priest was dressed in his customary all black shirt and pants. Around his neck was the white tab collar that distinguished him as a member of the Catholic clergy.

"Good evening, Father." The crowd responded in unison as though they were attending a Sunday mass.

"Thank you all for coming tonight. I think the size of the crowd tonight is a testament to how well-loved Amber McCloskey is in this town. I was honored when Jared asked if I would speak tonight and pray with you all. I want to start off the night by saying, if anyone out there has any information on the whereabouts of Amber, please come forward. If you are uncomfortable or frightened about speaking to a police officer, please come speak with me. I still spend most of my days over at St. Peter's in the gardens. I can relay information to the police and keep your identity between myself and God. Nobody ever really disappears without a trace. Somebody out here tonight *probably* knows something. You may have seen something that you didn't realize was important at the time, but now you might be thinking differently. Please, nothing is too insignificant. We just want Amber home safe."

Father Collins would turn 90 that November, and besides the white hair and beard and cane, one would never guess he was that old listening to him speak that night. He spoke slowly and deliberately without a hint of fatigue, as he might during one of his homilies. People liked and trusted him. When there was an event happening at the church he was always the first person to get his hands dirty. He ladled out bean soup during the annual church bazaar wearing a green apron with a leprechaun on it. He ran the children's Trunk or Treat every year at Halloween in the church parking lot, and spearheaded Toys for Tots every year in December. He was a pillar of the community in more ways than one, and for once in his very lengthy career he hoped to use that to his advantage and draw information out of somebody for Amber's safe return.

Jaime bit her lip and pushed back the emotions that were crawling to the surface. If her and Flynn were right, Amber was never coming home. She was long gone, to where Jaime still didn't know or really care to know.

Father Collins spoke for a few minutes more, thanking several people for helping put the night together, to the church for donating the candles that were now being passed around and lit, to everyone who had left a picture or flower at the memorial under the scoreboard. Finally, he wanted to turn the microphone over to Jared and let him speak.

Jaime and Flynn watched as Jared, who was standing at the foot of the stage, leaned over to another man standing next to him and whispered something into his ear. The mystery man turned his head and whispered back, and then Jared took the stage. Neither of them could see exactly who the other man was, but he was older than the three of them. He was wearing what appeared to be khaki pants and a Hawk Ridge High School football windbreaker. Ah, they thought, another coach. The entire team was here wearing their jerseys in support of their quarterback coach, all the other coaches must be in attendance as well.

Jared stepped to the mic looking pale and nervous. *I guess if I had fed my wife to an ancient demon as sacrifice, and then had to face the rest of the town I'd be nervous too.* The thought amused Jaime and caused her to hide a chuckle behind a cough. At Flynn's confused look she whispered her thought to him, and he too caught a case of the chuckle coughs. They turned their attention back to the stage and listened to what the grieving husband had to say.

To Jaime, Jared looked like a man going up against the firing squad. Even from her position away from the stage, Jaime could see Jared's hands shake as he adjusted the microphone. When he spoke, his voice shook for a moment almost as much as his hands.

"Let me begin by thanking each one of you for taking time out of your busy lives to come here tonight. I think Amber would probably have been embarrassed by how many people showed up tonight in support of her. She was never one for a lot of attention, always preferred to be the one behind the camera instead of in front of it. But, I think she would have been extremely grateful as well. I think she would have gone around and hugged and thankful everyone individually. I hope you all will join me in continuing to pray for her safe return home. Thank you."

With that, he turned the stage back to Father Collins and hurried down the stairs back to where he had been originally standing. The older coach leaned over and whispered something in his ear, to which Jared nodded slowly in response to. Father Collins bowed his head began his prayer.

"Heavenly Father. We gather tonight to ask for the safe return of our wife, daughter, and friend Amber McCloskey. If someone has taken Amber, Father, please let them know all we wish is for Amber to be home with us. If Amber has wandered, Father, please let her know we miss her dearly and that all will be forgiven when she is home with her family. May your Holy Spirit guide her home, in Jesus' name. Amen."

Flynn motioned for Jaime to step away from the crowd with him.

"Tell me you caught that," he burst out once they had stepped behind one of the concession stands.

"Past tense," Jaime replied. "He talked about Amber in past tense. Someone should only do that if –"

"They know the person is already dead," Flynn finished.

"So, now what?" Jaime asked. "Mixing up tenses isn't exactly hard evidence or a confession, especially when you're as dimwitted as that moron. We have to get over to the historical society and find that contract before anyone else disappears."

Flynn nodded.

"I think we're going to have to split up for this part." Flynn suggested. "I'm not a huge fan of the idea, but I think we need to keep eyes on Jared as much as possible while one of us searches the historical society. I don't want to be digging around down there, and have him surprise us."

"You're right. If he gets wind of what we're up to, he could set that thing on us. What's your plan for getting into the historical society? I think breaking and entering is frowned upon usually."

"Tomorrow morning, we walk in the front door. Tell whoever's working that we're doing some family research, and we'd like to spend some time looking into newspapers, files, pictures. I bet that would be more than enough to get some alone time."

"Okay, so while you're doing that, I'll be keeping tabs on Jared wherever he goes."

Flynn raised his eyebrows at this.

"You sure you want to be the one to follow him?" he asked gently.

"Flynn, I love you, but you stick out like a sore thumb. You're the biggest guy in town, and I think Jared might spot you following him. At least if someone does recognize me, I can use the excuse that it's my first-time home in years, and I'm just hitting up all the old spots."

Flynn rubbed a hand over the back of his neck as he listened to what she had to say. She was right, and he knew it.

"Fine, but we keep in contact all day. Updates at least every hour, if not more. I also don't want you confronting him alone."

Jaime responded with a salute and a smile.

"I hereby swear not to be a dumbass and confront the psychotic killer alone, unless someone is in imminent danger of becoming the demon's next sacrifice."

Flynn knocked her in the shoulder for being a smart-ass, and then chuckled.

"Come on," he said peeking around the corner of the stand. "Let's get out of here."

The crowd was now singing a hymn that Jaime faintly recognized from her time spent in church growing up. She couldn't place the name of it, but she remembered it was one that she had always kind of liked. She felt a warm, not unwelcome feeling wash over her for a second and then it was gone. They quietly made their way to the gates, but not before making sure that Jared was still standing in front of the stage. They had almost made it to the gates when a voice spoke up from somewhere in the shadows.

"I guess you thought showing your face here tonight would make up for all the trouble you caused in our lives years ago."

Shit, Jaime thought. This was exactly what she was hoping to avoid. She turned just in time to see Amber's mom step out from behind one of the concession stands. She had always been a thin woman, but the stress of losing her only daughter made her look almost skeletal. Her face was pale, and her eyes were red from the exorbitant amount of crying she had been doing lately. Her chestnut colored hair, same as Amber's, Jaime thought absentmindedly, was pulled tightly back into a bun. Even with just the stadium lighting Jaime could see streaks of gray beginning to show.

Immediately, Jaime wanted to blow up at this woman. Tell her that Amber going missing happened because she pushed her daughter into a life that Amber had never wanted, that she didn't belong in. She could feel Flynn tense up next to her, getting ready to drag her out into the parking lot before things could get ugly. But she surprised all three of them with what she came out of her mouth.

"I'm sorry that you're going through this, nobody should have to not know where their loved one has disappeared to. And I'm sorry for whatever trouble I caused to you and your husband years ago. It was never my intention to drive a wedge between you and your daughter. I just hoped that one day you would see that I was somebody Amber deserved to have in her life. Someone who really cared about her."

Amber's mom was ready for a fight, so when Jaime uttered those last words she looked like she had just been slapped in the face.

"How dare you accuse me of not caring about my daughter!" she spat. Her voice rose with each word. Jaime could practically feel the fire and venom that coated each word. "I love my daughter! I loved her enough to make sure she got away from you so you couldn't drag her into everlasting damnation with you!"

A few heads were beginning to turn their way. Fuck. They had to get out of here now. A confrontation with this woman was the last thing Jaime wanted. She had already gotten enough attention to last a lifetime tonight. Flynn placed a hand on Jaime's shoulder, not to hold her back but, just enough pressure to let her know she needed to be careful with whatever it was she said and did next.

"The only thing I ever did to your daughter was love her, and if that makes me a sinner in your eyes, then so fucking be it. If that's what your "God" tells you is wrong, and that my soul is doomed to be damned, then I want nothing to do with what your so-called salvation might be."

Without waiting for a response, Jaime spun away and strode out the gates with Flynn close on her heels. She understood that there was nothing she could ever say to Amber's mom that would make her see her as anything but an abomination, but it also felt damn good to finally tell this woman what she had always felt.

Flynn followed Jaime back to the Jeep, wanting to give her some distance to calm down after the confrontation with Amber's mom. Flynn had known Jaime a long time, since first grade as a matter of fact, and he had always known she was different in a way. For the longest time, he couldn't put his finger on exactly what it was. He was only six when they met after all. But as the years went on, and they grew closer, and they each learned to trust one another, Flynn began putting the pieces together. So, when Jaime came out to Flynn in the seventh grade on a Friday night while shooting basketball in his driveway, scared to death of what he might say, Flynn just laughed and asked her if she really thought he didn't already know. The look of relief on her face made him laugh even harder, and pull her in for one of his bone crushing hugs.

"You are the smartest and prettiest girl in the middle school, Jai, you really think I would have waited this long to make a move if I thought you were straight?" He asked still laughing.

Jaime jabbed him in the ribs in response, and then hugged him even tighter.

"Thank you," she whispered. "Please keep this between us for now? You know how small towns are and all."

"Hey, of course. I know you can take care of yourself and all, I've got bruises from wrestling you to prove that," he joked. A second later, however, his face grew dark and serious. "But if anyone ever gives you a hard time about this, I guarantee it will be the first and last time."

Flynn kept his promise to Jaime and never said anything to anyone else about what she had confided in him. It wasn't until about three weeks before school let out for summer the following year that he was somewhat tricked into semi-divulging Jaime's secret.

Thirteen

May 2001 – Hawk Ridge Middle School

The last bell of the day had already rung going on twenty minutes ago now. Summer vacation was right around the corner and everyone could feel it, especially on days like today. The sun had been out all day, and not a cloud was in sight. The school thermometer located just outside the front office doors read in the upper sixties all day, and was currently trying to break seventy. For springtime in Pennsylvania, which would occasionally receive those freak spring, one more for good measure snowstorms, this meant it was time to break out the shorts and t-shirts.

The halls were already devoid of any human life, (except one), everyone anxious to get out on this beautiful Friday afternoon and get their weekend started. Even most of the teachers had vamoosed, leaving their lesson plans for Sunday night, or Monday morning for some. The lone figure in an empty hall, Flynn sat propped against a grouping of lockers outside the eighth grade English classroom, waiting for his weekend to begin. From his position, he could vaguely make out the conversation that was occurring between his best friend and the English teacher, Mr. Meltzer. Three weeks left in the year and Jaime was still concerned about getting an A on her final research paper of the year, when they could have already been halfway home. This girl was going to give him an ulcer, he thought with a chuckle.

Knowing Jaime as well as he did, he knew this 'quick question,' as she had called it, could quickly turn into a forty-five minute conversation. To keep himself occupied, he reached into his backpack and pulled out the latest Stephen King book, *Dreamcatcher.*

People were always surprised how much Flynn, who was considered a 'jock' by many, loved to read. His own home library was quite impressive, especially for an eighth grader who was just supposed to be a dumb jock. Engrossed in his latest literary adventure, he didn't hear the footsteps make their way down the hall to where he was sitting, nor did he notice the figure standing over him until they cleared their throat, and nearly gave him a heart attack.

"Sorry," the newcomer said. "I didn't mean to scare you, but you were so focused on your book."

"Hey, no biggie," Flynn responded. A second later he realized who had snuck up on him, and was in addition to being startled also confused. "Amber. Hey. What are you still doing here?"

Amber Davidson was one of the most popular girls in the eighth grade. Not only was she the eighth-grade class president, she had straight A's, was involved in almost every club, was the lead in every school play and musical, sang in the choir, and was even an excellent soccer player. Flynn also had to admit that she was incredibly pretty, and she could have any guy that she wanted. The only problem was that her parents were strict Catholic, and had forbid her from dating anyone until she was sixteen. Bummer, he remembered thinking when he had found this out last year.

"Well," she began slowly. "I was hoping you could help me."

Suddenly, her eyes began darting back and forth, searching for anyone lingering who might overhear this conversation. She may have startled Flynn, but she was clearly the one who was spooked now.

"I need you to take a message to someone for me, and you cannot tell another soul who it's going to, or what it's about. My parents control a lot of what goes on in my life, but controlling my dating life, or who I even talk to –." Here she broke off for a second to collect her thoughts. "I don't want to live my life wondering 'what if' or 'what could have been.' You know what I mean?"

Holy shit. Amber Davidson, the most popular girl in school, had come to him, lowly jock Flynn Baygo, for help with her love life.

"Sure," he managed to stutter out. "Yeah, of course I'll help. Who do you need me to take the message to?"

Amber paused for a second, she looked like she was contemplating running away and never speaking of this moment again, but then Flynn could see Amber steel herself as she reached into her purse to retrieve something. Out came a regular, white, everyday envelope that had a name scribbled on the front. When she handed it over to Flynn and he could see the name, he couldn't stop his jaw from dropping wide open.

Jaime

"I'm going to be honest," Flynn said after picking his jaw up from the floor. "I did not see that one coming."

"I mean, I don't even know if she would welcome a letter from, someone, like me, but I figured if anyone would know it would be you. But, like, if she's not, you know, you can just burn that thing, and –,"

"Amber," Flynn broke in. "You're rambling. And don't worry. Jaime will be okay getting this, from someone like you."

It appeared like a hundred-pound weight had been lifted from her shoulders when she heard those words. Her face lit up, and she no longer looked like she might burst into tears at any moment.

"Wow. Okay. Uhm, I gave directions in there for what to do in the event she might like to meet up, or whatever. So, hopefully I see you again soon?"

"Yeah, cool. I'll make sure she gets this."

Amber nodded once more, and then turned to head home for the weekend.

Once she rounded the corner and was gone from sight, Flynn looked down at the envelope in his hands. He couldn't wait to watch Jaime open this, he thought full of excitement.

"What'cha grinning at?"

In his excitement, Flynn didn't hear Jaime exit the classroom. He knew this wasn't the place to have this conversation, so he jumped up, grabbed Jaime, and began pulling her to the school doors.

"Come on! I'll show you when we get to my house."

Jaime opened her mouth to protest, and then decided to close it and just go along with it. Once Flynn got a hold on something, it was impossible to get him off it until he willingly relented. She knew if she even attempted to drag her heels he could, and would, sling her over his shoulder and sprint the rest of the way to his house. Sometimes it was just easier to let him get everything out of his system, and let him calm down on his own. He could be like a Golden Retriever with his favorite bone. She was genuinely curious though as to what he had been looking at when she walked out of Mr. Meltzer's room.

What usually took about twenty-five minutes to walk home from the middle school to

Flynn's house only took fifteen that day since Flynn had them power walking the entire way. By the time they were making their way up the front stairs to the porch, Jaime, who was in decent enough shape, was struggling to catch her breath trying to keep up with Flynn's longer stride.

"Whatever it is must be worth it if you're going to end up giving me heat stroke over it."

"You go down to the basement," he said completely ignoring her complaints. "I'll grab us a couple waters."

"Boy is going to give me an ulcer." Jaime mumbled making her way down the stairs.

Less than a minute later, Flynn came bounding down the stairs with two water bottles in hand.

"Okay, so what gives?" Jaime asked before guzzling down almost half of one of the bottles.

"No more questions for now. Just read this."

Flynn pulled the envelope from the pocket of his shorts and held it out in front of Jaime's face. She immediately looked baffled, and opened her mouth to ask another question despite Flynn's urging.

"I have no clue what it says," he said cutting her off. "I agreed to deliver the message and that's what I'm doing."

Without another word, Jaime plucked the envelope from his hand, tore it open, and began to read.

Flynn watched as Jaime's eyes skimmed the first couple of lines, face still full of skepticism about what she might find. Little by little though, her eyes grew wider and her lips curled into a smile. By the time she had reached the bottom of the note and found the name of the note writer, both cheeks had turned a rosy pink, and her smile threatened to split her face in half.

"You're not shitting me, right?" She asked, nervous about what Flynn's answer might be. "This isn't some kind of sick joke?"

"I swear it's not. I talked with Amber myself right before you came out of Meltzer's room. This isn't a game to her. She was serious about the whole thing, I could see it on her face." After a few agonizing silent seconds, scared he might have made a mistake, he added, "So, what do you think?"

"I think," Jaime started, picking and choosing her words carefully. "You have to help me write a response that's not going to make me sound like a dumbass."

Hearing this Flynn broke into a smile so wide Jaime was sure he'd pull a muscle in his face.

"Yes!" He cried, pumping his fist. "Grab a notebook out of the desk, let's start brainstorming what your response is going to be."

Fourteen

December 2009 – Pennsylvania

    Christmastime was always a pretty big deal in Jaime's family growing up. The weekend following Thanksgiving was always the designated decorating day in the Strait household. Boxes marked 'Christmas' were dragged out of the attic, lights were strung up on the front of the house, and even the Christmas tree was erected. This year had been no different, and Jaime was very pleased to be done her last final and be home for winter break so she could enjoy the festivities that went with the holiday season.

    There was still a week to go before the twenty-fifth of December, but all over town people were kicking off the celebration. That night downtown Hawk Ridge was hosting a Santa's Village complete with horse drawn carriage rides, hot chocolate, caroling, craft vendors, and even the big man himself, Santa Claus. The Strait family had only arrived minutes ago, and while Jaime's parents ran ahead to grab some hot chocolate, Jaime hung back near the Creamery where her and Flynn had made plans to meet up. Flynn was running a little late tonight thanks to work, but Jaime was happy to wait for him.

Christmas always seemed to brighten her mood about coming home from college. It was a cool night, but not frigid, especially not by Pennsylvania winter standards. It had recently snowed the previous weekend, and there was still about an inch covering parts of the streets and sidewalks. Jaime was enjoying listening to the festive music that was wafting out of the Historical Society. Th two-story brick building had garland hanging from the second story windows, and a nine-foot Douglas Fir could be seen through the giant plate glass window on the first floor. Decorated in multi-colored lights, beads, and probably close to two hundred glass ornaments, it was a photo-op that many families couldn't pass up. Suddenly, a voice broke through the last lines of O' Come All Ye' Faithful, and the night got a lot colder.

"Well, hey stranger. Long time no see. You still off chasing those college dreams?"

Jaime would have recognized that voice anywhere. She had lain awake on countless nights imagining it saying something else. Steeling herself, Jaime turned and tried to stretch her mouth into a pleasant smile.

Jaime hadn't seen Amber since high school graduation, but she was just as Jaime remembered. Chestnut hair hung down past her shoulders in soft waves. *A little bit longer than the last time I saw her,* Jaime thought offhand. She was dressed in jeans, a thick purple sweater, and knee high black boots. Draped over her arm was a black pea coat she could throw on later when it got a little colder. Amber's parents had been very strict and diligent about keeping them apart. Jaime had tried to text Amber a few times the summer after high school, but either Amber's number had been changed, her parents had been monitoring the messages, or she simply wasn't interested in answering anymore.

"Hey, yourself," Jaime responded trying to keep her voice light and friendly. She wanted to ask if her parents were around somewhere, but managed to hold her tongue. This was no place to have it out. "It's senior year, one more semester and I'll be done."

Amber nodded, and offered her congratulations. There was a moment of silence, and the two stood there staring at each other. Neither exactly sure what to say next. Finally, Jaime broke the silence with the only thing she could think of.

"So, what have you been up to lately? You going to school?"

Amber responded with a smile that didn't reach her eyes, and then stuck out her left hand that until now, had been hidden by the coat, for Jaime to see the giant rock that now resided on her ring finger.

"Got engaged last month." Her voice was soft, but Jaime could hear the excitement underneath.

Jaime tried to keep her reaction to a minimum, but she could feel her eyes bulge in their sockets, her stomach drop, and her mouth fall open. *Well, this is unexpected.*

"Wow, congratulations! Anyone I know?" She tried to sound sincere, but she could hear the contempt in her voice, and if she was being honest with herself, the jealousy as well.

"Jared McCloskey."

Hearing that name made the earth spin under Jaime's feet, and her vision to go blurry for a second. This time Jaime didn't even try to keep the look of confusion and disgust off her face.

"You're kidding, right?"

Amber seemed to be expecting this reaction, and immediately tried to smooth things over.

"He's not the same guy we knew in high school, Jaime. He's changed. He's a really sweet guy when you get to know him."

"And I'm guessing your parents are over the moon about this? Finally found yourself a nice boy to settle down with."

There it was. The sarcasm was out of her mouth before she could even think to reel it back in. The words resonated though, and Amber did her best to cover up the hurt.

"This has nothing to do with my parents, but yes. They're thrilled for Jared and me."

"If they are, I guess I should be too. Your mom always treated me so well and everything. She knows exactly what happiness looks like."

Amber paused to gather her words before responding to this comment.

"I'm not the same girl you knew in high school, Jaime. I'm not that sinner anymore. I didn't know what I was doing. My parents helped me find God, and He's shown me the right way to live my life. If you can't come to terms with that, then I guess this is good-bye. Have a good life, Jai."

And before Jaime could get another word out, Amber was gone into the crowd. A few minutes later, Flynn found Jaime staring at the empty spot on the sidewalk, hands clenched into fists as she tried not to cry. Jaime knew how childish it was to be mad at Amber, but she couldn't help it. She had always hoped that maybe one-day Amber would stand up to her parents, and tell them that no amount of holy water and prayers would change her. But now, with that new addition on her finger, it seemed that dream would always remain just that.

Fifteen

When they were nearly back to the Jeep, Jaime came to a stop in the middle of the parking lot. For a second, Flynn thought she might turn to head back to the field to give Amber's mom one more parting shot. Instead, she just stood there clenching and unclenching her fists, taking deep breaths, holding them for a long beat, and then releasing them through her nose.

"I didn't come here to cause a scene tonight, but damn that felt good," she finally said.

"It was long overdue too," Flynn agreed. He paused while Jaime took deep breaths and got herself under control, then he opened his arms. "Come here."

Immediately Jaime fell into his embrace, comforted for the moment.

"I'm proud of you for handling that so well."

"What?" She asked a little confused. "I didn't exactly hold my tongue as well as I should have."

"Yeah, but you didn't slug her like I know you always wanted to."

At this, they both broke into laughter. It felt strange to be laughing after such a somber evening, but it also felt right. Once they both calmed down, Flynn placed a chaste kiss on the top of Jaime's head.

"We're going to figure this out," he promised. "No one else is going to get hurt."

"But how can you –."

The sound of sirens somewhere in the distance silenced her. They shot each other a 'now what?' look, ran the rest of the way to the

Jeep, and peeled out to see if they could find where the disturbance was coming from.

"You see anything yet?" Flynn asked as he swung the Jeep onto one of the side streets near the school.

"No, but whatever is happening must be close. Those sirens were close enough that my ears are still ringing." Jaime responded.

Suddenly, Flynn slammed on the brakes and the Jeep came to a stop in the middle of Elm Street. Even in the dark, Jaime could see the wheels turning in his mind. He had an idea.

"What're you thinking?" Jaime asked after a few seconds of letting him contemplate in silence.

"Jackson Street." Flynn answered without another word.

"The furthest street out over on this side of town. The street closest to the woods." Jaime filled in the blanks, and felt a chill crawl up her spine as she spoke.

Less than two minutes later the pair could see blue lights appear in the night sky over the rooftops of the homes on Pine Street. The Jeep made the final turn from Pine onto Jackson, and into a scene of chaos.

Parked in front of 411 Jackson Street, Jaime counted four police cars and a black SUV. All were empty of any occupants. Standing on the porch of the two-story home was girl of about eighteen years of age in hysterics. Trying to calm her down was a female officer who had been three years ahead of Jaime and Flynn in high school. Her name wouldn't come immediately to Jaime. Later when she asked Flynn he would tell her it was Carmen Houlihan, who still held the school record for the 400-meter dash in track and field. Flynn would also tell Jaime that in high school he had been almost positive Carmen had been sleeping with Mr. Kellen, the senior math teacher.

By the sound of things and the number of flashlight beams, Jaime guessed there were about another half a dozen officers in and around the backyard of the house. One of the officers rounded the house as Jaime and Flynn were approaching the scene from where they had parked about half a block away. They didn't want to get in anybody's way, but they were also curious as to what was going on. They recognized the officer immediately as Flynn's Uncle, and Flynn shot a quick wave to him. When Uncle Danny saw them approaching, he held up a finger as if to say, give me a minute. Flynn and Jaime stood out on the sidewalk waiting patiently while watching the girl on the porch. Her long, brown hair was completely disheveled from her running her hands through it. Jaime found herself wishing she could go up and offer her a hair tie. The girl wore jeans and a Hawk Ridge High School sweatshirt, but still appeared to be shivering violently. She was still crying, but had since calmed down slightly. Jaime wouldn't have been surprised if the poor girl was simply tiring herself out. Finally, Uncle Danny placed the radio back in the car and turned to the pair.

"One hell of a night already," he began tiredly before offering Jaime a smile. "Good to see you again, Jai. Even if it's not under the best circumstances." He was a little older, and a little grayer around the ears, but he was pretty much exactly how Jaime had remembered him.

"What happened here?" Flynn asked. "Girl looks like she's been through hell."

Uncle Danny looked at them, took a breath, and then rubbed a hand over his eyes before answering.

"Girl was babysitting a young boy, nine-year-old Jacob Millsap. Apparently, she's over here at least twice a month watching the kid while his parents go out. They were out in the backyard playing catch when she said they heard something rustling around in the trees. Figured it was just a squirrel or rabbit at first. Then –." Here he paused to look over his shoulder at the house. "Then, she said she saw antlers just inside the tree line."

Jaime's heart skipped a beat, and then began pounding in her chest. *I knew it. Call it ESP, call it a lucky guess, call it whatever the fuck you want,* Jaime thought. Her mouth suddenly felt like it was full of cotton. She ran her tongue over her lips trying to produce some saliva, but couldn't. For a second it truly felt like her entire throat would dry up and she would choke to death on air.

"Girl said Jacob got excited when he saw the antlers, and he took off to get a closer look. She said she yelled after him, but he was gone into the trees before she could get a hold of him. She took off behind him, calling his name, but when she got to the trees, he had vanished into thin air. She said she thought he was playing a trick on her, so she searched the trees thinking he had scaled one and was waiting to drop down and scare her. But he wasn't anywhere to be found. She ran back to the house and called the police. She thinks maybe someone had been hiding in the trees watching them, waiting to snatch the kid up. We've been trying to tell her it's more likely he just ran a little too far, got turned around, and got lost. Girl's worked herself into hysterics. Can't seem to calm her down. Parents of the kid are on their way home."

"You really think he just got lost in the woods?" Flynn asked his Uncle. His voice was full of skepticism and all three of them heard it.

"That's what we're going with until we have any other evidence telling us otherwise. There's no reason to believe this was an abduction. I have a few officers out combing the area, but we'll probably have to wait until first light to really get the search going."

Jaime and Flynn nodded in agreement.

"I'm not sure what the girl saw in the trees, but I want the two of you to go home and stay there for the night. If there is a kidnapper running around, which I seriously doubt, I want the roads as clear of cars as possible. It's going to be a long night, and an even longer day tomorrow."

The three said their goodbyes, and Jaime and Flynn jumped in the Jeep to head back to the house. The ride was silent until they pulled into the driveway and Flynn killed the engine.

"No one is going to see Jacob ever again, are they?" Jaime asked quietly, despite knowing the answer already.

"No," Flynn answered softly. "I don't think so."

Word of the disappearance spread around town before the sun had even come up and it seemed every able-bodied citizen wanted to be out searching for Jacob. Police actually had to turn people away from the search parties. They were worried too many people in the woods might make too much noise and Jacob's cries for help would go unheard. Immediately there was talk of Amber and Jacob's disappearances being connected somehow, but no one could think of any solid theory for someone wanting to take them both.

For the time being, the plan of Flynn searching the historical society and Jaime tailing Jared remained the same. Flynn arrived at the door of the historical society just as it was being unlocked. He explained that he needed to do some research, and was given basically free roam of the building. There was no conceivable way he was going to cover the entire building in one day, but at least he had a believable story as to why he was spending so much time there.

Jaime's end of the plan was less appealing, especially for her. Following one of her tormentors from high school around all day wasn't on the top of her to do list, but like she told Flynn, she blended in better than he did. Even if people were stopping to talk with her about how she was doing, it was a plausible story as to why she was sitting on a bench downtown or grabbing a soda at the drug store.

She just hoped that Jared didn't realize everywhere he went, she also went.

The morning trudged forward for the pair. One digging through piles of dusty and sometimes moldy newspapers, maps, pictures, and letters while the other tailed one of the most well-known faces in town. Every hour as promised, one would send the other an update of how they were doing and the other would respond with their progress, or lack thereof. Finally, at around one-thirty that afternoon Jaime followed Jared to the high school. It was time for him to begin his football practice prep for the day. This is where Jaime would leave him and head over to the historical society to give Flynn a hand until the place closed at five.

Jaime watched from the driver's seat of her Mustang as Jared made his way into the football team's locker rooms to start his day as the quarterback coach. He had played the position himself when they were in high school, and almost everyone had loved him for it. Even though a lot of people seemed to forget how bad he was under center. Jaime remembered the homecoming game her senior year. Flynn and she decided, what the hell, let's go see us get our asses kicked. And boy were they not disappointed. The Golden Bears of Mahanoy Area four towns over had whooped them 56-10. Jared had at least two interceptions and if she remembered correctly, a handful of fumbles. Flynn had spent most of the night commentating in his fake announcer's voice every missed opportunity or bad play the Hawks made, and by the end of the night Jaime was in tears from laughing so hard.

    Suddenly, a voice snapped her out of her trip down memory lane and smacked the smile that had formed right off her face. She sat unmoving in her seat, desperately attempting not to react.

"Jaime Strait," the voice began. "Who the hell let you back in this town?"

The tone was meant to be joking, but Jaime could also hear the contempt beneath the words, and it was just as cocky as she remembered.

Sixteen

November 2002 – Hawk Ridge High School

The Wednesday before Thanksgiving break was always a fun day at Hawk Ridge High School. Everyone was looking forward to Thanksgiving the next day, and having a long weekend away from school. Most of the teachers even shuffled their learning plans around that day to include games, movies, or free days into the curriculum.

It was nearing the end of the day, and Jaime only had one more class to survive to make it to break. Despite this, she couldn't help but feel her anxiety creep up inside her. She was doing well in biology, but her and the teacher never saw eye to eye, and lately it was bad. Ever since her incident last month, Mr. Gallagher, was being more of an asshole to her than usual. Making matters worse, Jared also shared this period with her. And even though he was dumb as a rock when it came to this stuff, Mr. Gallagher was one of the football coaches, so Jared never had to worry come test day, or report card time. It infuriated Jaime to no end, but she could never get her hands on actual proof that he was changing Jared's grades to make them look better.

The previous day he had promised that they would do something 'fun' to celebrate the upcoming holiday since this class, he claimed, was doing the best out of all his classes, and that it wouldn't be graded. There were rumors going around that morning that they would be dissecting a turkey in honor of Thanksgiving. Once she heard this, Jaime began looking forward to her last period for once. This would be way better than dissecting a frog, or a worm, or something lame.

The second bell had just sounded, meaning everyone should have been in their final period classroom awaiting to begin class, but Mr. Gallagher was nowhere to be found. Even Jared, notorious for being several minutes late, and never receiving a writeup, had no idea where he was. Jaime shrugged it off, thinking every minute he's not here is one minute closer to Thanksgiving break. She opened her mouth to ask Flynn a question pertaining to another class, when the door to the classroom sprung open.

Mr. Gallagher appeared pushing what looked to be a large operating table of sorts. Whatever was on it was covered in several layers of plastic and couldn't be seen, but there was an awful smell evident from the moment the door opened. It smelled strangely like pickles. *Yeah, maybe if the pickles were left in the fridge for about a decade or so.*

"I know several of you were expecting to come in today and dissect a turkey in honor of Thanksgiving being tomorrow." He had rolled the table to a stop in front of the room, and was now beginning to rearrange some of the desks so they all could gather round. "Unfortunately, I do not have a turkey under all this plastic."

Hearing this, a few groans erupted from near the back of the room. Almost as if being egged on by the misery, Mr. Gallagher's normal toothy grin grew into something more of a sinister snarl.

"I do, however, have something under here to celebrate what happens the Monday after Thanksgiving. I know many of you will be out in your tree stands bright and early that day while the rest of us are enjoying our extra day off."

Jaime's eyes bulged in their sockets, and shot over to Flynn's. No way, they both communicated silently. The bastard.

He started unravelling some of the plastic while he continued talking.

"I also thought this would be an excellent time to help one of our students see what this animal looks like up close. Just in case she's ever chased by one again." To every other student it simply sounded like a funny joke, but Jaime could hear the malice in the biology teacher's voice. *He really fucking hates me,* Jaime thought.

The plastic crinkled as he peeled away the layers. The formaldehyde smell became stronger as each piece was peeled back until finally, it was so strong several pairs of eyes began to water, and Mr. Gallagher had to put on a surgical mask and goggles. The final piece of plastic was then pulled back to reveal an adult female deer lying motionless on the table. Several shouts of excitement arose from the students who were hunters who would be spending the Monday after Thanksgiving, the first day of deer season in Pennsylvania, hunting for their own one of these. Mr. Gallagher explained that he had come across this deer on Route 61 about a week ago after it just had been hit by a car. Knowing a good lesson when he saw one, he scooped it up and took it to his taxidermy buddy who preserved it for him until today.

Everyone proceeded to gather round the table, donning masks and goggles of their own in order to watch their biology teacher slice open the belly of the deer. He pointed out and described all the major organs and arteries inside the animal. He then had each student step forward to get a closer look, and practice their own hand at dissection. When Jaime's turn came around, several students snickered. Jared wasting no time in calling out.

"Hey, deer girl! Is this the one that chased you?"

She wanted to ask him if he knew the difference between male and female deer, but bit her tongue. She didn't want to give Mr. Gallagher any reason to keep her after class, or make things worse. She silently stepped forward, pulled her gloves on, and grabbed a scalpel. She could feel herself shaking, more out of anger than fear, but she refused to give Mr. Gallagher, Jared, or anyone else the chance to see and capitalize on it. She gritted her teeth under the mask, and did her part of the dissection, cutting out one of the lungs with precision that even some surgeons lack. Once the lung was free, she placed it on the tray with the rest of the organs that had been removed, placed her scalpel down, and returned to her spot standing beside Flynn near the back of the crowd of students. The grin that had been on

Mr. Gallagher's face fell and his eyes hardened when he saw that she wasn't going to have a mental breakdown, and that her cuts were even better than his. He covered his disappointment by quickly moving on to the next student and the next organ to be removed. The rest of the period passed without incident, and when the final bell rang for the day Jaime was relieved to be free of school for the next five days.

December 2003 – Hawk Ridge, Pennsylvania

It was tradition for Jaime's family to have Christmas dinner at her aunt's house, which was located about an hour outside of Hawk Ridge. The three of them would pile into the car early in the morning with a giant bowl of Mrs. Strait's mashed potatoes, and head off to spend the day eating too much, opening presents, and napping on the couch. Later that night, they would pile back in the car, make their way home, and then open the presents the three of them had gotten each other. Besides the one year of the Christmas Day snowstorm where they were forced to stay over at her aunt's house, they had enjoyed Christmas this way for as long as Jaime could remember. This year was no different, and around seven o'clock that night Jaime and her parents piled back into their Ford Escape and made the hour drive home listening to carols on the radio, discussing the gifts they had received that afternoon, and teasing one another with the gifts they were still about to open.

Jaime was distracted trying to figure out what one package sitting in their living room could be when her dad pulled the SUV onto their street and entered the final stretch to their house. Suddenly, she was jarred from her thoughts when her dad slammed on the brakes and her mom let out a shriek to raise the dead.

Even a year after her incident in the woods, her first thoughts were, it's come back to finish the job. *It waited until I thought I was safe and in the clear, but now it's come to take me.* Her eyes bulged from their sockets, as she strained to see out the windshield from the backseat. Her dad had thrown the SUV into park and had his door open before Jaime could yell to him to stay inside. She struggled to get her own seatbelt unbuckled, fighting it while it locked and held her in place. When she managed to free herself, she spilled out onto to the street. A moment later, her eyes landed upon what the headlights had illuminated.

There, in the middle of the driveway, lay the body of a dead deer. Had it not have been for the bullet hole through the doe's neck, one might have thought it had just fallen asleep and was resting for a minute.

"Cheryl," Mr. Strait called from his position bending over the animal. "Call the police. Somebody put this here on purpose."

Jaime was quickly hustled inside the house, where she was told to stay until further notice. Twenty minutes later a police cruiser and a Chevy Silverado pulled up to the Strait driveway. Uncle Danny emerged from the driver's side of the Silverado, and Flynn from the passenger's side. Flynn's entire family was over at his house relaxing after dinner watching *It's a Wonderful Life* when Uncle Danny's work phone rang. When Flynn realized the call was about Jaime's house, he ignored the protests from his mom, and jumped into his Uncle's truck with him. Flynn took one look at the carcass in the driveway, and sprinted up to the house to find his best friend. He burst through the front door into a dark house, Jaime hadn't bothered to turn any lights on yet. His eyes scanned the kitchen, and when they didn't find anything he moved into the living room. There, on the couch, is where he found a Jaime-like shape plopped down on the cushions. Slowly, as not to scare her, Flynn lowered himself so he was sitting next to her.

"Hey," he began. "It's me. My Uncle was still at the house when he got the call on his cell."

"This is never going to stop, is it?" came the muffled response. "I'm always going to be deer girl to this town."

Flynn wasn't sure how to respond to this. He wanted to say that sooner or later, people would forget about it. That one day, it would be something they'd be able to laugh at, but then he remembered how cruel people could be. Especially people in a small town who had nothing else going for themselves, those who chose to bring others down with them. So instead of words that both he and Jaime wouldn't believe, he opted to place a hand on her back until his Uncle came to talk with her.

"There's no way for you to find out who put that deer in our driveway, is there?" Jaime asked as she sat up to face Uncle Danny.

Uncle Danny scrubbed a hand down his face, and let out a pained breath.

"Probably not, kid." Uncle Danny spat in disgust. "The bullet it was killed with was dug out, so there's no way to match it to anything. You have any idea who might want to do something like this?"

"Oh, I can probably come up with a few names," Jaime said thinking immediately of some of the guys from school. Jared at the top of the list.

"Well, you write them down for me, and I'll see what I can turn up. Maybe one of these idiots said something to someone they shouldn't have. You take it easy, and enjoy the rest of your Christmas. Let me handle this mess."

Seventeen

She turned herself in her seat and saw the owner of the voice. She had recognized it right away, just as she had Jared's, but the sight of him still made her clench her fists and jaw. She was glad that she had her sunglasses on so he couldn't see the disdain and, if she was being honest with herself, the little bit of fear that had crept up in her eyes.

"Didn't realize I needed to have my passport stamped to come back home," she responded, trying to keep her voice even and light. Upon closer inspection, she realized this was who Jared had been whispering with the previous night at the vigil.

"Jared said that you were back in town the other day at practice. Said you were back to pay your respects for Amber. Damn shame, isn't it?"

She hadn't seen Mr. Gallagher, since she had graduated high school. No complaints from her. She fucking hating the bastard.

"Yeah," Jaime ground out. "A tragedy really. I'm still holding out hope that someone finds her alive."

"The longer this goes on, the less I'm believing that's a real possibility. Jared's been a real trooper throughout this whole thing though. Hasn't missed a practice or a meeting since it happened. I think football helps take his mind off it. Even just for a few hours. What are you doing down here at the school now?"

Shit. Was that suspicion in his voice? Jaime guessed it could be possible that Jared had co-conspirators in this. He might have lookouts all over town, her cover could have been blown hours ago. Jared might have known she was following him the whole time.

"Just hitting up some of the old spots," she said trying to sound nonchalant. "I haven't been home in seven years, so it's nice to sometimes just go and sit somewhere and reminisce."

"I'm surprised you came back, even for Amber. If I remember correctly, you always hated this place."

Yes, Jaime thought. *A large part thanks to you.*

"Things change over the years." she gritted out through clenched teeth. "Sometimes a little time away is all you need to get a clearer picture about a place."

She needed to get out of here before she said or did something she would come to regret. This guy always knew how to push her buttons, and he apparently still had a good grasp on it.

He nodded as if he knew exactly what she was talking about.

"Well, I have to get to practice. Big game coming up this Friday night. See you around, Jaime."

"Bye, Mr. Gallagher."

"Oh, please. It's Chris for my former students." He called back over his shoulder as he walked towards the field.

Jaime watched him walk away and into the locker rooms, waited two minutes, and then turned the ignition and turned the wheels towards the historical society.

"He really said 'a damn shame'?" Flynn asked exasperated. Jaime had just relayed her conversation with Chris to him, and he was just as suspicious of him as she had been.

"It was like he was talking about losing a football game instead of a human being."

"So, you're thinking that Chris is in on this with Jared? That he knows about the contract and the demon?"

"I think it's a solid possibility. Jared was never burdened with an overabundance of intelligence so he easily could have let it slip over a couple drinks with Chris about his family's history with the town."

Flynn raised his eyebrows and tilted his head in consideration.

"Two people who know what's going on is going to make this more dangerous for us. If they even suspect that we know, we could be the next ones on the demon's hit list."

"We need to find that contract now." Jaime said flipping through an old photo album full of newspaper clippings. In her head she added, *if it even actually exists*. "You make any headway here this morning?"

"After about the first two hours of searching on my own, I realized that it was going to take us weeks, maybe even months to go through everything by hand. I decided we had to narrow this down. I asked one of the nice ladies out front where they kept everything on the founding of the town. That's when they brought me upstairs to this room. Said that everything on the first hundred years of the town should be found in this room, give or take a year or so. Since then, I've managed to clear one wall of files and information."

"Couldn't it be possible though that if someone did put it in here, they purposefully hid it somewhere where we wouldn't think to look? Say, in with things from the last decade or so?"

Flynn nodded as if he was expecting her to think of that idea.

"I thought the same thing. We have to start somewhere though, and I figured this was as good a place as any."

"We better get going then. It's only a matter of time before someone learns that we're poking around in here, and word gets back to Tweedle Dee and Tweedle Dum."

For the next three and a half hours Jaime and Flynn flipped through every box, album, bag, and drawer in the room. Twice they thought they had found what they were looking for, but both times it turned out to be land contracts between the town and someone's small business. Five o'clock rolled around, and they were no closer to finding the contract than they were at the beginning of the day. They left the building and made the drive back to Flynn's house feeling tired, dusty, and defeated.

"It's gotta be in another room there, right?" Jaime asked as they sat down at the kitchen table to go over plan B. "Someone must have moved it to a different room to keep it safe. One of Jared's ancestors must have been scared that someone would come along and figure it out, so they moved the contract to throw them, us, off the scent."

Flynn was quiet for a few moments, deep in thought. They had to have missed something somewhere.

"Okay," he began slowly. "Let's say you're right. Let's say the contract was in the historical society at one point, maybe even in that very room we were in today. Kinkaid surmised that the reason it was put in the historical society to begin with, was because it would guarantee its safety."

Jaime nodded in complete agreement.

"We all figured that nothing would ever get tossed out accidentally, and it could sit undetected for centuries."

"Right. So why would someone move it from there? What location could be safer for a piece of paper than the historical society?" He asked.

"We assumed that the historical society would always be the safest place for the contract. And maybe it was a hundred years ago, but not anymore."

When Flynn shot her a look of confusion, she continued not wanting to lose her train of thought.

"Flynn, think about it. Things people find important change over time."

"Like nowadays people care less about their town's history and more about how many likes they get on their social media posts." He threw out, starting to understand. "So, if that's the case, what place in town fits the bill? It's still got to be a place where Jared could get to it fairly easily, but secure enough that no one else can just stumble upon it."

"We find out what this town holds close to its heart, and we find the contract."

"How many things could this town love?" Flynn asked. "A little hole in the wall place like this. What do these people hold above all else?"

Suddenly, after a few seconds of thought they blurted out together,

"The football team!"

"Holy shit!" Flynn exclaimed.

"That's gotta be it!" Jaime cried. "You think it's buried under the field somewhere?"

"No," Flynn ran a hand over the stubble that had formed on his jaw, thinking. "No, they wouldn't put it anywhere near the field. Even if they put it in a box or chest it'd be way too easy for the ground's crew to dig it up accidently.

There's way too much traffic on and around the field. They'd put it somewhere only they have access to, but not the locker room or weight room. Still too easy for someone to stumble on it."

The pair sat in silence, thinking hard for any iota of an idea of where the contract could be. They were so close to the finish line, to ending their town's curse forever. They could make it so that no one else had to experience their friend or child vanish without a trace. Suddenly, Flynn started as if struck by something. His head whipped up and his eyes bulged in their sockets.

"Holy shit," he breathed out. "I think I know where it is. It's the only place that makes sense. It's safe enough that nobody it going to accidently come upon it, only a few people have access to it, but it's still in plain fucking sight."

"Where the hell do you find a place like that around a high school?" Jaime asked. Her heart was pounding so hard she could feel it in her ears. This could be the big break they needed.

"The football trophy case." He gushed. "It makes perfect sense. The only people I ever saw open that case when we were in school were the coaches of the football team. I doubt that's changed over the years. They were always nuts about keeping that thing in check. I remember once seeing one of the coaches inspecting the janitor's cleaning supplies when he was cleaning the glass."

"That thing is full of trophies and plaques from decades ago too," Jaime added excitedly. "Which means they never get rid of anything out of that thing. I would bet money that's where the contract is! Now, how the hell do we get it out of there? We can't just go busting the thing open with a hammer, can we?"

Flynn chuckled and then answered,

"No, as much as I would love to, I think Jared would have that demon, or the police, after us immediately if we did that. But there has to be a way for us to get at that trophy case without causing a raucous."

"Do they still hold town pep rallies at the school before home games on Friday nights?" Jaime asked. She was getting excited again because she felt she had the makings of a plan forming.

Flynn paused a second to think, and then lit up. He felt like he was on the same page with her. That just might work.

"Hey, yeah! They do!"

"What if we show up for the pep rally Friday? Nothing suspicious about that. A good chunk of the town is there every week. It'd be easy to blend in and disappear in the crowd." Jaime plotted.

"Pep rally ends, we hang back, wait until the place clears, and then go for the trophy case. Everyone will head to the field, and we should have free roam of the place. The only problem that I foresee, is how we're going to get into the case without smashing it."

"We need a key." Jaime sighed, knowing full well that no one who had one would ever willingly let them 'borrow' it. "Your fingers still as sticky as they used to be?"

Flynn let out a hearty laugh at this. He knew exactly what event Jaime was referencing. It was their junior year of high school, and for whatever reason Jared and his football playing asshat friends were being extra-large asshats to everyone they didn't like that week. They, of course, hadn't messed with Flynn, because he was a tank, but they had gone after a few of his other friends. The final straw, however, came when they went after Jaime.

Flynn, Jaime, Jared, and a few Jared's friends all shared the same English class that year. The latest assignment was a research project on an author whose works they enjoyed reading. Jaime and Flynn had both immediately known what authors they wanted to write their papers on, Shirley Jackson and Stephen King, respectively. Jared, who had bitched and moaned endlessly when the paper had been assigned, had yet to decide on an author. Mainly because in his mind, 'only faggots read books.'

That particular morning in class, their teacher, Mr. Hill, had taken them to the school library to gather some material for their papers. Flynn and Jaime had set up shop at a table together where they could spread everything out in front of them, and pick and choose what they wanted to keep and what they wanted to return.

Jaime had just printed out several articles on Jackson's gothic writing, her upbringing, and even a few letters the *New York Times* had received in response to Jackson's short story *The Lottery.* All of the desktops were connected to one central printer that was located across the room from where the tables sat. Jaime had just retrieved the articles, hot off the press, from the printer and was navigating her way through the tangle of tables and chairs filled with other students back to her seat. She was so focused on where she was going, that she never saw the foot sneak its way out from under one of the tables. By the time she realized what had happened, she was already sprawled across the floor with all her papers scattered every which way. A voice she recognized as Jared's rang out from above her.

"Watch where you're going Deer Girl! People are trying to work here! I thought deer were supposed to be graceful creatures!"

His entire table of asshats laughed hysterically at this, and Jaime felt her face turn red in embarrassment and anger. Instead of punching his lights out like she really wanted to, and in turn gaining an in-school suspension for the rest of the day, she gathered her papers up as fast as she could and shuffled her way back to her table. She plopped down in the seat next to Flynn and kept her eyes down, trained on the table. She could feel her face burning, and tears stinging the back of her eyes. *This might be worse than the deer pictures in my locker,* she contemplated.

She could feel Flynn fuming next to her, but they both knew he wouldn't do anything here. He knew Jaime could handle herself, and he didn't want to make things worse by starting a fight. Instead, he began forming a plan in his head.

Two periods later, it was gym class. Juniors were still required to change into gym uniforms in separate locker rooms. After they changed, they could partake in whatever physical activity they desired, as long as they were doing something active. Flynn changed much slower than he normally would, waiting until all the other guys had made their way out of the locker room and back into the gym. That was when he made his way over to Jared and his friends' lockers, and made off with the clothes they wore to school that morning.

The theft was discovered when it was time to change back into street clothes. Jared pitched a fit that someone had stolen all their clothes, but found little sympathy from his classmates. The entire locker room was searched, including all the lockers, but the clothes were nowhere to be found since Flynn had stashed them in a place only he and a handful of the other basketball players knew about.

One day after basketball practice the previous year, someone accidently knocked one of the ceiling panels loose with a ball. Not wanting to get in trouble, they quickly moved it back into place and forgot it ever happened. Flynn, however, used this spot to his advantage that day and hid the clothes in this secret spot in the ceiling.

The consensus on the missing clothes was that someone had used the second entrance that led from one of the school hallways into the locker room while class was going on, and that the clothes were probably somewhere else by now. Jared demanded a search of every locker in the school, and he of course got his way. Every student stood by their locker while teachers looked through them, but none of the missing clothes turned up from that search. It seemed the only thing to do was have the boys wear their gym uniforms for the rest of the day. The uniforms consisted of bright red cotton shorts with the word HAWKS printed in gold on the left leg, and a school bus yellow shirt, that faded to a more off-yellow once you washed it a few times. Across the front of the shirt was a picture of a hawk in red outline with the words HAWK RIDGE HIGH SCHOOL. Every student, and most of the teachers agreed, that they were the ugliest things ever.

    Jared and the others sulked for the rest of the day as their other friends laughed and made fun of them, but the tormenting that week stopped. Not to say it stopped forever, because asshats will be asshats, but it did take a while for them to pick back up. After that day, Jared also began keeping his clothes on the bleachers during gym class to make sure they never did another disappearing act.

Flynn never admitted to anyone what he did, except for Jaime when she figured it out on their drive home from school that day. Flynn was worried for a second that she would be mad at him for fighting her battles for her, but instead, she just smiled and reached over and gave his hand that wasn't on the steering wheel a squeeze.

"I can't remember," Jaime laughed. "Did you ever return the clothes, or are they still rotting in the ceiling?"

"Still in the ceiling," Flynn smirked. "It's one of the great mysteries of Hawk Ridge High School, what happened to those clothes. I would've done it again, but I didn't want to push my luck. I should've hid their entire backpacks that day."

"But you still think you have it in you to swipe a key from someone?"

"I think I can work something out," he answered. "None of the coaches are ever at the pep rally though, so we'll have to get one before Friday. If it was me, I'd want that key with me at all times. I'd probably stick it right on my key ring with my house and car keys."

"And the keys to the locker and weight rooms. It's going to be a challenge to figure out what key goes with what lock, and do it quickly."

"It might not be," Flynn said after thinking for a moment. "If the football trophy case is anything like the basketball one, the key will be smaller than a normal house or door key. That would narrow the choices down considerably. Now we just need a plan to pocket the key without Jared knowing."

Suddenly, the doorbell to the house rang. It was so unexpected that both of them jumped, and Jaime actually bit her tongue.

"You order a pizza or something?" She asked Flynn as he made his way towards the door.

"Not unless someone ordered for me," he answered. Neither of them even realized that they had begun whispering.

Flynn slunk to the door and pulled back the small curtain covering the window to see who was standing on the other side. Upon seeing who was there, he dropped the curtain like it was on fire. He wheeled around and looked at Jaime with wide eyes.

"We may have a problem here," he stuttered. "Get all this stuff out of here now. Move it into the hall closet."

"What's going on?" Jaime squeaked, jumping up and knocking her chair backwards.

"Jared is standing out on the porch."

Eighteen

Jaime's eyes flew open as wide as Flynn's when she heard this.

"Quick!" Flynn cried. "Just get everything off the table. I'll keep him outside as long as I can."

Jaime flew into action and began grabbing handfuls of papers, shoveling them into the box Gary Kinkaid had given them. Once everything was stuffed back into the box, she rushed it away to the hall closet, and hid it behind Flynn's jackets and numerous pairs of sneakers.

As soon as Flynn was confident that the box was out of sight, he unlocked and swung the door open. Jared had moved to stand near the edge of the porch, his back turned to the house, and he was looking out on the street watching the evening traffic drive by. The sun was beginning to lower itself in the sky, and a steady breeze had picked up filling the air with a slight chill. Flynn felt goosebumps rise on his arms, unsure if they were actually from the weather. Flynn waited a second to see how Jared would react to him opening the door. He for sure thought that Jared would rush him, so he braced himself for an attack. What actually happened was not what Flynn was expecting in the slightest.

"I think I may be in a little bit of trouble." came the small, shaky voice.

When Jared turned around with tears in his eyes, Flynn was completely stumped as to what was happening.

"What the hell are you talking about? What are you doing here?" Flynn asked gripping the doorframe so tightly his knuckles were beginning to turn white.

Jaime had crept up behind Flynn and was now pressed against his back listening intently to what they were saying. Her hands were buried in Flynn's shirt, gripping it tightly to keep them from shaking.

"Please," he pleaded. "I need your help. Both of you. I think I'm mixed up in something bad."

Flynn held his ground, despite the performance from the man on his porch. He was not convinced that this was all an act, and Jared was just waiting for them to drop their guard.

"You have never given us any reason to trust you all the years we've known you. Why in the hell should that change now? You have thirty seconds to convince us, or I'm going to come out there and beat the shit out of you."

This was only partially true. Yes, they didn't trust Jared as far as they could throw him, but they also needed his key. And if they could lull him into thinking they were helping him, maybe they could pick it off him while his guard was down. But they were also curious as to what Jared was doing on Flynn's front porch. They had known Jared a long time, and he had never been the dramatic type nor one to ever look so helpless.

"Jaime," he called out softly. "I know you're in there, and I know you saw something fifteen years ago, I know I treated you terribly afterwards, and I will understand completely if you don't want to hear anything that I have to say. But please, I know what it was, and I know who's responsible for it."

Flynn turned around to Jaime.

"We have to let him in," Jaime whispered. "Maybe we were wrong. Maybe he's not the one in control of it, but perhaps he does know who is."

"And if he's lying?" Flynn asked, voice just below a whisper, still a little skeptical.

"Then you beat the shit out of him."

Flynn chuckled, but he knew Jaime was right. They needed Jared, if just for the moment. Without another word, Flynn turned back around and opened the door fully to Jared, welcoming him into his home. Jaime pulled out one of the chairs at the kitchen table and motioned for him to sit. Her and Flynn sat down opposite him, letting him know that they were still on opposing teams for the moment.

The room fell into an uncomfortable silence for what felt like forever. Finally, after collecting his thoughts Jared began to speak.

"Hawk Ridge has a secret. It has to do with Amber's disappearance, it has to do with that Millsap kid's disappearance, and it has to do with what you saw in the woods fifteen years ago, Jaime."

"We know all about the disappearances in Hawk Ridge." Jaime broke in. "Every fifteen years people go missing and they're never found."

Jared's mouth fell open in dismay.

"How –." He began before being cut off by Flynn.

"We've done our homework."

Hearing this, Jared snapped his mouth shut. He blinked hard once to clear his head, and then began talking again.

"I am partially responsible for Amber's disappearance. I made a rash decision, and I have to live with it, however long or short that time may be. I can't go back and undo any of the awful things I took part in, but I can't let this continue any longer. I don't know what it is exactly that's taking these people. I'm sure you two have a better grasp on it than I ever will. But, I need your help in stopping him. If he knew I was here right now, we'd all be dead for sure."

"Him?" Jaime inquired. "You know who's in control of this thing?"

Jared nodded and then,

"I didn't know back in high school if that's what you're wondering. I only just found out when Amber went missing. I've always respected him, but he also always kind of scared me in a way, you know? Even in high school. He always looked at some of the guys weird at practices. I can't explain it, I never could, but it always seemed like he was trying to figure out who of the guys he could take in a fight, or something like that."

"Who Jared? Who is in control of this thing?" Flynn asked raising his voice as he went.

"It's Coach Gallagher. Mr. Gallagher from biology. This thing has apparently been passed down in his family, kind of like how some families pass down pocket watches. Except the Gallagher family passes down a fucking monster that I guess eats people."

"And he told you this?" Jaime demanded. "He told you his family has been in control of the thing that takes people every fifteen years?"

"He told me everything, mostly everything, I guess. He said it's for the good of the town. Said that the town's guaranteed well-being is worth a few lives every so often."

"And I'm guessing that he played a big part in Amber's disappearance. Is that right?" Jaime was fuming. She could tell that Jared was scared, but the fear he felt now didn't cleanse him of what he had done to Amber.

"I swear, I didn't know the whole story until after Amber disappeared. I had no idea that's what was going to happen."

"Start from the beginning," Flynn said, trying to ease the situation. He hated the guy as much as Jaime did, but right now they needed the information he had. "Don't leave a single thing out."

"I'm not exactly sure when it started. Amber and I had been married for five years. The first three, maybe even four years, were very happy years. Then, it seemed everything just began to come apart at the seams. We were fighting almost every day, we'd go to work in the morning without saying good-bye. Stupid things like that. Then, things started getting bad. We both started saying some pretty nasty things to the other. Every time we opened our mouths, an argument or an insult came out. She started saying how much of a mistake it was to marry me. How she didn't love me, but that her parents forced her into this relationship to begin with. She began bringing you up more and more, Jaime. She would say some nights how the two of you should have just run away after high school. How it was a mistake for her to let her parents dictate her life for all these years."

Jaime listened quietly, but with an ever-growing rage. She forced herself to sit on her hands so that she wouldn't be tempted to jump up and slug Jared right across the mouth. There would be time for that later, she told herself.

"About a month ago, Coach Gallagher, Chris, realized that something was wrong one day at practice. He invited me out for a few drinks that night, and I ended up spilling everything to him. All the fighting, and second guessing, and frustration I felt came pouring out. He listened to everything I had to say without saying a word of his own. Once I was done, he sat there like he was deep in thought for a few moments. He had this look on his face that pissed me off, but also kind of scared me, you know? Like he knew something that I didn't. I knew he was toying with me, but I was also curious. He goes on to tell me that he has a way for me to wipe the slate clean, and that I'd never have to get my hands dirty. He said that no one would ever be able to connect me to it, even though I was Amber's husband. He said he had it all worked out."

"You had to have known that he was talking about getting rid of her." Flynn broke in. He had forced himself to sit on his hands so he wouldn't be tempted to jump up and nail this idiot right between the eyes.

"No, not at first. At first, I thought he was just talking about scaring her. Maybe if she just had the fear of God put into her, she'd be easier to live with. That we wouldn't fight anymore, and that we both could be happy. I told him, sure, let's do it. I asked him what he needed from me, and he said nothing. Said that he had it all taken care of, but that we both needed an alibi for when it went down."

"That was when you remembered the scrimmage coming up," Jaime snapped. She always knew this guy was dirt, but this, this put him lower than pond scum in her mind. "There'd be people all over the place who could say without a doubt where you two were when Amber went missing. It would be ironclad. But, how did you get her out of the stands by herself? What if she wouldn't have gone to the bathroom when she did?"

"I'll admit we had to go on a little faith with that," Jared confessed. "But, I had a pretty good idea she'd leave the stands at some point and go off on her own. Amber started smoking around the time our arguments started picking up. I was the only person who knew. She didn't want anyone else seeing her with them, especially her parents. Her grandfather had died of lung cancer when she was younger, and they made her swear on his grave when she was a teenager to never pick up the habit. I figured she'd walk out and around the back of the stadium at some point. I told Chris as much, and he said, that would work. That for it to work the person had to be off by themselves."

Jaime nodded. Amber had told her years ago about the awful battle with cancer her grandfather had endured. Her parents were nuts over keeping her away from cigarettes and cigars. Amber always told them they had nothing to worry about; that she hated the smell anyway. *I guess, some people could get over just about anything when they were desperate.*

"Alright, so game ends and you go home and realize Amber's missing. Then what?"

Flynn had a good idea of everything that happened next. But, he still wanted to hear it from the horse's mouth.

"Chris told me to wait a little bit after I'd gotten home to call the police to report her missing. He said to tell them I figured she had went somewhere with a friend after the game, but that I was starting to get worried that she still wasn't home. When she still wasn't back the next morning is when I think I realized that she wasn't coming home. That was when I met Chris at the football field and he told me everything about his family secret. How when his like fifth great-grandmother and her sister, helped found the town, they knew it would need a protector of sorts. So, they made a deal. A deal where every fifteen years this – this demon, he called it, would come and take as many people as it saw fit in exchange for protection of the town and its citizens."

"I'm guessing this is when you realized you were dealing with a raging psychopath, who probably comes from a long line of raging psychopaths?" Jaime growled out.

"That's not how he sees himself," Jared said shaking his head. "He truly believes that he hasn't done anything wrong, that no one in his family has. He kept saying that the good of the town outweighs the lives that are taken every fifteen years. And that he never even has to get his hands dirty if he doesn't want to. Everything is already taken care of."

"So he's more of the Charles Manson type than Ted Bundy." Flynn snapped. "That doesn't make him any less guilty of what's happened. He must have some type of control over it. Does he pick all its victims? Or only some of the ones he wants to get rid of?"

"From what he told me, this thing picks its own meals. But, he also said the name can pick sacrifices if they want. That's how he got it to take Amber. How he manages to do it, that I don't know. He didn't go into details, he just said for him to offer a sacrifice the person has to be alone, or the demon will wait until they're alone."

"This thing has to be bound to him and his family somehow. Did he ever mention how?"

"He called it The Settlement. I'm guessing it's a piece of paper, the actual piece of paper, his ancestors signed when they made the deal that has been passed down through the ranks of his family. Apparently, when you take over possession of it, you have to sign your name in your own blood. It made me lightheaded just to hear him talk about it."

"And you never saw this Settlement?" Jaime asked. She was still furious with Jared, but at least they were getting something useful from him.

"No, but he told me where he keeps it."

"Let me guess," Flynn stepped in. "The trophy case at school?"

The way Jared's eyes widened and his mouth fell open let them know that they had had the right place in mind.

"I knew I should have copied off you two back in high school instead of Lee Coolidge." He paused and ran both hands down over his face. There were black circles under both eyes, and it appeared that he hadn't had a good night's sleep since this whole thing began. "I'm assuming you two have a plan already cooked up?"

Jaime and Flynn gave each other worried looks before answering.

"Stay here," Flynn said to Jared. "We need to discuss some things first."

The pair moved to stand in the living room where they could keep an eye on their visitor, but were confident enough that they wouldn't be overheard.

"What are you thinking?" Flynn asked keeping his eyes on Jared. "Do you think we can trust him enough to use him in the plan? Or, do you think he's playing us? That Chris isn't involved at all, and he's the psychopath."

Jaime collected her thoughts for several moments before answering. She trained her eyes on the man who was sitting at Flynn's kitchen table. She had known Jared for most of her life. He had treated her like dirt for a good portion of it. He only ever looked out for himself and his best interests, but right now he looked like a shell of who he used to be. The dark circles were evident under his bloodshot eyes. This was not the same man who had filled her locker with hundreds of deer pictures, or the one who embarrassed her in front of the entire library.

"I don't believe that he's playing us," she began slowly. "If he is, he's doing an incredible job of playing the part. I also don't think he's smart enough to pull that kind of charade off. I think we need a leap of faith right about now."

Flynn shifted his gaze and met her eyes. Finally, he nodded satisfied that Jaime truly believed what she was saying.

Once back in the kitchen, Flynn and Jaime laid out the rough plan they had come up with not thirty minutes prior. Jared sat and listened intently, more intently than they had ever seen him listen to anything in high school. Once they were finished, they asked if he thought they could pull it off that Friday night while most the town was a stone's throw away.

"It's a great plan," he said sounding quite impressed. "It's a perfect plan actually, but there's only one thing I think we need to change."

"What would that be?" Jaime asked, ready to jump on the defensive.

"I don't think we can wait until Friday. I think we need to do this as soon as possible. I don't like the idea of knowing what's going on while Chris is still out there. Every night I lay down to sleep I wonder if this is the night that Chris realizes he can't have another person out there who knows what he knows. I'm terrified that he's going to send that thing after me at any given moment."

"Right now, then," Jaime blurted out, startling the two guys. "Let's finish this tonight. What's Chris doing right now? Is he anywhere near the school?"

"Practice ended a couple hours ago. He probably watched some film for a while, but he should be home by now. He lives on the other side of town. Even if he was out standing on his porch he would never see us drive by on our way to the school."

"How are we going to get into the school now? Aren't the doors locked all the time nowadays? And what about the security cameras?" Flynn asked. He didn't like rushing into this half-cocked. At least on Friday they'd have a legitimate excuse to be in the school. "The three of us sneaking around after hours is going to look pretty suspicious."

"I have a key that gets me in one of the side entrances. All the coaches have them in case we need access to the athletic department's office and there's no one in the main office to buzz us in. It wouldn't be hard to explain why I'm there after hours to anyone who might watch the cameras, but why you two are there is another story."

"Hey, I might have a solution for that," Jaime perked up. "What if we make it seem like you're letting us in to use the basketball court? They still do that, right?"

Jared nodded. "Every Thursday night they open the doors for people to come shoot. But I've seen a lot of coaches and teachers bring people in on other nights."

"That'll work," Flynn agreed. "But what about why we're opening up the trophy case?"

"There's only one camera in that hallway with the case, and it's been busted for about a year now. They think some kid shot it out with a slingshot or something, but they never found who did it. Plus, it's not all that rare for one of the coaches to go in and move things around, or even take something for it to be cleaned. I don't think we'll be questioned too much on that if it comes up."

Twenty minutes later after packing a duffel bag with some appropriate basketball playing attire, just in case someone did stop them, the now trio jumped into Flynn's Jeep and took off for the school.

Nineteen

The parking lot at the school was completely deserted when they pulled into it. It seemed that luck was on their side, for the moment, at least. They still had a way to go before their work was finished for the night.

They parked right out front, so it didn't look like they were up to something if someone did drive by and question why they were there. The door Jared had the key to was located about ten yards around the left side of the building. It was an unassuming steel door with no window, easy to overlook if someone didn't know it was there.

Jared shoved his key into the lock and leaned his shoulder into the door so it would allow the key to turn. It wasn't uncommon for the door to go weeks, or months even, without use, and would get stuck when someone did try to use it. Once the door was opened and they were inside, their anxiety increased. The air somehow felt thicker inside than out, despite of the air conditioning. It was almost as if the school knew what they were there to do.

It occurred suddenly to Jaime that they must look like a strange group. All three of them had been well known during their high school days. Jared for being the quarterback, although not even a decent one. Flynn had been the Captain of the basketball team his junior and senior years. And Jaime for seeing a monster in the woods. Anyone who knew them during their teenage years would have bet their life savings that the three of them would never have come together to accomplish anything. Now that she thought about it, if they were indeed spotted someone might have a difficult time believing that Jared agreed to bring them here to use the gym. Jaime's mind then jumped to the question of who was the most nervous right about now.

She, of course, had nothing else to lose, in this town, other than her life. That ship had sailed fifteen years ago when she burst through those police department doors. In some weird way, this thought seemed to ease some of her nerves. Flynn didn't get nervous, she thought. Flynn got focused, and got shit done. It was what made him such a good basketball player in high school. He had at least half a dozen game winning or game tying shots under his belt. And this was about to be the biggest one of all.

It was definitely Jared, she mused. Jared, who had been a terrible football player, but everyone always loved a quarterback, and apparently a quarterback coach as well. Sure, he had lost his wife during all of this, but the town rallied around him and just wanted to help him through his difficult time. He had no idea what he was getting himself into when Chris offered to wipe the slate clean for him. He still probably doesn't fully grasp everything that's happened, Jaime thought. Out of the three of them, Jared was the one with the most to lose if this went south in a hurry.

The gym sat in what was the direct center of the school on the first floor. There were four separate entrances, all from four separate hallways. It had been designed this way to help evacuations in case there was ever an emergency while the gym was full. It also came in handy when there were assemblies held, and helped students pile in and out faster and more ordered. The football trophy case sat in the hallway directly across from the door they had entered. By cutting through the gym, they would exit out the other side right in front of it. Flynn popped open the first gym door, and they all filed in one after the other. The main lights that hung from the ceiling were all off, but a few small lights located on the walls were always kept on. Once their eyes adjusted to the loss of light, they moved across the floor with no problem. Jaime got to the door first, and hit the metal bar that ran across it, spilling them out into the hallway.

The trophy case ran for about twenty feet on its wall, and stood about another five feet high with three shelves situated inside. At first glance, one would be tricked into thinking it was packed full of trophies, medals, and plaques. One's eyes would be drawn to the two Pennsylvania State Class A Championship trophies from the 70s. Then the plaque listing the players who had accomplished 1,000 yards rushing and receiving would come next. After that, however, nothing else was really as exciting. Upon closer inspection, one would see how spread out everything was arranged. They'd notice how trophies didn't really need two feet of space on either side of them, but that they were set up that way to take up more space. They'd wonder why there was so much equipment in it as well, and realize it was because there were no more trophies to display.

The three of them stood staring at the case not moving for a minute. Three pairs of eyes darted every which way trying to decipher where the Settlement might be kept. Hundreds of years of disappearances could be avenged, and no more families would have to live without knowing what happened to their loved one if they could just find and destroy a stupid piece of paper.

"Did Chris give you any notion as to where in the trophy case it might be?" Jaime asked, her eyes never leaving the case.

Jared frowned, tilted his head, and squinted before answering.

"Nothing specific, just that it's in the trophy case. He said he likes keeping it right under everybody's noses without them having a clue that it's there."

"I guess we just look everywhere then," Jaime responded. She hadn't expected it to be that easy, but she still had to give it a try. "Go ahead and open it up."

Jared stepped forward, reached into his pocket, and brought his keyring back out. The keys clinked together as his hands shook like leaves in a windstorm, so much so that he dropped them before he could even find the key he needed. In the empty hallway, the keys sounded like glass shattering when they hit the floor, and all three of them cringed at the sound.

"Guess we're all a little on edge," Flynn said trying to lighten the mood. But he was right. They all wanted to get this done as fast as possible. None of them would admit it out loud, but they couldn't get over the idea that they might not be alone in the building.

Finally, Jared got his hands under control enough to pick out the key he needed. He moved to the left side of the glass box, where the lock had always been located, and then stopped. His face scrunched up, and he tilted his head again. Jaime thought he looked like a big dumb dog in that moment, and had to stifle a laugh.

"What's wrong?" Flynn asked. Jaime didn't like the way his voice sounded when he spoke. It sounded nervous. Flynn was never nervous, and that made Jaime nervous. They both moved to stand behind Jared and see what he was looking at.

"The fucking lock has been changed," Jared growled. "This wasn't like this a couple weeks ago when I was here."

"Chris changed it after he told you where the Settlement was," Jaime moaned. "I guess he doesn't trust you as much as you thought."

"Now what?" Jared croaked. "We can't smash the case, can we?"

"No, we'd have to smash the entire thing and I don't foresee that ending well for any of us," Flynn mused. "We're going to have to crack the combination."

"That could take hours!" Jared complained. "We don't have that kind of time."

"Maybe not," Flynn pondered, looking closely at the lock. "My dad had a lock like this when I was a kid. He used it on his tool cabinet out in the garage. Most combination locks come with their own combinations, but this one, whoever buys the lock gets to choose their own numbers for the combination."

"But even if we figure out what numbers he used, it's going to take forever to crack the order in which they're entered into the lock," Jared pointed out.

"Maybe not," Jaime perked up. "I have an idea, come on!"

Without waiting for a response, she took off down the hallway. She hadn't been in this school in over a decade, but she still knew exactly where she was going. Nothing seemed to ever change in this town, and she was hoping the same held for the school. Two right turns down the hallways, and she skidded to a stop in front of the room she was searching for. Upon seeing the name on the door, MR. GALLAGHER, she knew she was in the right place. She pressed her face against the glass of the door's window and strained her eyes to see inside. The lights were all off, and the sun was getting low in the sky, but the remaining rays allowed for just enough light for her to see what she needed to see.

"I knew it!" she cried. "Nothing ever changes in this damn town."

Seeing their confused faces, she moved away from the window, and motioned for them to look.

"Do you remember what Chris had hanging above his desk while we were in school?" she asked while the guys had their faces pressed against the glass.

"Yeah, his high school, college, and club football jerseys," Jared responded. "I should know even better than you guys."

"You are a genius!" Flynn exclaimed as he spun around. "That's got to be it!"

"You guys lost me," Jared complained.

"The jerseys," Jaime explained. "There's three of them, with three numbers."

Jared's face lit up once he realized what Jaime was getting at.

"This actually might work!" he called out.

"14…23…34," Flynn read off from his position in front of the door.

Once back at the trophy case, Jaime stepped up and spun the lock, stopping on all the appropriate numbers. They weren't positive this was the answer, but at least they had somewhere to start.

"Right 34," she whispered to herself, concentrating on not going a single click past where she needed to go. She lined up the number with the main dash line, paused for second, and then tugged. The lock came free, and all three of them released breaths they didn't realize they had been holding. Now that the lock was off, it allowed them to slide the panels of glass of the case back and forth freely. They'd start at one end of the case searching for the Settlement, and work their way down, moving the panels back and forth as needed.

"Let's be smart about this," Jaime cautioned. "Try not to move too many things at once. That way we'll remember where everything goes. I don't want anyone to know that someone was in here because a football is facing the wrong direction.

They started at the end closest to the lock. They each took a turn picking something up out of the case and thoroughly examining it. They tugged on every piece of trophies, looking for secret compartments. They checked behind plaques, and looked for secret panels that might slide away on them. They tried to crack open footballs and cleats, and even checked to make sure it wasn't sewn into one of the jerseys.

They were almost halfway through the case, and their confidence was waning every time they picked something up and it didn't have the Settlement in it. They began wondering if Chris had lied, and that he was still the only person who knew where it was hidden.

"Maybe he buried it in a chest, like pirate's treasure," Jared mused.

No, thought Jaime. He'd want to be able to go to it any time he wanted. Sometimes the answer wasn't nearly as complicated as people made it out to be. Answers to riddles tended to be simple and right in front of your face. Overthinking was what got people into trouble.

She ignored Jared's belief in buried treasure, and grabbed the next thing off the wall. It was a team picture framed from 1996. Weird, she thought. It was a well-known fact that the Hawk Ridge football team had been awful during the decade of the 90's, worse than even the present day team. Even when they had been in high school, whenever someone would bomb a test, they'd make a joke about the score at least being higher than the number of points scored by the football team in the 90's. Why in the hell would there be a picture of one of those teams in the trophy case?

She showed the picture to the guys, and posed her question.

"That doesn't make any sense," Jared puzzled. "During some of the ass reamings in the locker rooms, coaches always brought those teams up. Used to scream at us that we were going to end up worse than they had been, which wasn't true, but it sure always did light a fire under us. We were always told that the trophy case was for winners. No second-place trophies belonged in there. I can't imagine how that picture would have made its way in here."

Jaime held the picture up closer to her face and examined the faces in the picture more closely. She didn't recognize any of them at first glance, so she lowered her eyes to the list of names typed up at the bottom. Nothing jumped out at her in the first two lines, and then, there it was. Third line down, sixth name over. CHRISTOPHER GALLAGHER, SENIOR. Jaime's heart pounded against her ribcage, and she began to shake all over.

Slowly, as to not drop it, she turned the frame over. The back slid out of the frame easily, and she placed that aside. Underneath that she found a piece of cardboard. She wanted to turn the frame over again and let everything fall out, but she forced herself to go slow. With shaking hands, she lifted the cardboard out, and what she found underneath made her breath catch in her throat.

Situated between the picture and the cardboard was another smaller piece of paper. It was about the size of a page out of a pocket-sized paperback novel, and appeared to be made of parchment paper. There was nothing written on the side that Jaime could see, so she steeled herself, and carefully lifted one corner of the yellowish-brown paper. The moment her fingers touched the sheet, Jaime could feel her skin break out into gooseflesh. To Jaime it felt warm and leather like, with almost a human skin feel. She could feel both guys pressed against her back, anxious to see if she had found what they were looking for. All three unknowingly crinkled their noses simultaneously. None of them knew it, but what they were smelling was the faint odor of sulfur. Like she was pulling a band-aid off her leg, Jaime flipped the paper over to see what was on the other side.

The writing on the other side was faded from the years gone by. Jaime leaned her face down, and squinted her eyes hard to make out what the swirls of ink said. The writing was in some elaborate type of cursive, and would have been difficult to read if the ink had been fresh, but now that it was so worn down, it was almost impossible to decipher the whole thing. They each took a turn reading through it, trying to make out a word here and there. They finally decided it read something like,

'I hereby swear to serve and protect this town of Hawk Ridge by any means necessary for survival. I will give my breath for this town, so that the future may thrive.'

Below that, was several signatures. The one was indecipherable, it looked like a mess of scribbles, and was in black ink. The ones that came underneath that one were readable, however. And they were all written in red. *Elizabeth Muldoon. Charlotte Muldoon. David Gallagher. John Gallagher. Peter Gallagher. Christopher Gallagher.*

"Muldoon," Jared said, seeming to try out how it sounded on his lips. "Hey, I've seen that name on some kind of family crest thing at

Chris' house. He once said it was an old family name."

"I bet that name shows up somewhere on Kinkaid's lists," Flynn said looking at Jaime. "We just never connected it to Chris because it disappeared when they got married."

"And we were so focused on something else," Jaime's eyes shifted to Jared for a second.

Flynn winced and nodded in agreement. They both felt like idiots for letting their former prejudices cloud their judgement. If Jared would have never come to them, they'd still be on his tail, and they probably never would've cracked the combination lock.

Jared didn't seem to notice that they were talking about him. He was still staring intently at the Settlement.

"I can't imagine signing my name in blood. Makes me want to hurl just thinking about it."

Jaime couldn't help herself, and burst into laughter at this admission. And once she started, she couldn't seem to stop. Soon she had Flynn and Jared laughing along with her. They laughed at Jared's hurl comment, and then Jaime thought again of how no one they went to high school with would believe the three of them were working together, and she began to laugh all over again. They all laughed for what seemed like twenty minutes, until tears poured out of their eyes, and their sides ached. Finally, they got themselves under control. Then they all looked down at the paper, and then back up at each other's faces.

"Sooo," Jared started. "Now what do we do? We probably shouldn't hang around here much longer."

"I guess it's time we burn this thing," Jaime answered as she stared down at the root of all the disappearances. "We still have no idea if it's going to work, but it's a good place to start."

"Wait," Flynn jumped in. "What if it's not fire? Let's think about it for a second before we do something we can't take back. Chris put this thing in the back of a picture frame next to another piece of paper. If the school would have ever caught fire, there's no way this thing would survive. It's got to be something else."

"What if it's got nothing to do with the paper itself?" Jaime threw out. "What if it's more about the name on the paper instead? What if there must be a name on the paper for the demon to be active? There's several names on the Settlement, all written in blood, but why?"

Flynn made a motion for her to continue, he thought he knew where she was going with this, but he didn't want to interrupt her thought process.

"What if when the person whose name is the latest on the list gets older, or close to death, or they just don't want the responsibility anymore, in order for the protection of the town to continue, and the fifteen-year cycle to stay intact, they need someone else to take it over? There needs to be a name on the paper of an able-bodied, live human being. I'm just theorizing here, but I bet that if the Settlement is destroyed, but the person who signed it is not, nothing changes. I'd also be willing to bet that the demon can conjure up another Settlement no problem, and have the next person in line sign that one instead of the original."

"That's great and all," Jared griped. "But what does any of that mean for us? How do we get rid of the demon?"

Flynn and Jaime looked at one another, trying to silently decide who should be the one to say it. Finally, Flynn took a deep breath, turned to the guy who he had always wanted to punch in the face and blurted out,

"It means we're going to have to kill Chris."

Twenty

"Hey, did you hear what I said?" Flynn questioned after Jared had no reaction to the revelation that they were going to have to kill his former football coach, and now friend.

"I heard," Jared replied. His voice held no trace of fear or trepidation. It was oddly calm, and it made Jaime and Flynn nervous. "Do you really think that will put a stop to this?"

"I have no idea," Jaime responded honestly. "But right now, it's the only play we got."

"Okay," Jared finally said after a few moments of silence. "How are we going to do it?"

"I don't think this is the right place to have this conversation," Flynn jumped in. "Let's get this case closed, and get out of here before a janitor or someone finds us here discussing murder."

At this, Jaime picked up the Settlement, carefully rolled it up, and placed it in her jacket pocket. Once the picture was back in the trophy case, they slid the glass panels closed and Flynn snapped the lock back on. They hoped that they put everything back where it belonged, and that nobody would notice if anything was different. They had no idea that it wouldn't even matter in a few short hours.

Outside in the parking lot, the Jeep was still the only vehicle to be found. They all breathed a collective sigh of relief that no one had driven by and thought it strange for one car to be parked at the school at this hour. Just before climbing into the passenger's seat, Jaime looked across the parking lot to the football stadium. That Friday the entire stadium would be filled with most of the town cheering for their hometown team. They'd eat their cheese fries and wave their red and gold flags and cheer for a team that might win four games that season, oblivious that one of the coaches of that team was a psychopath who had an ancient evil tethered to him. But Jaime had a feeling that if the citizens of Hawk Ridge ever found out what had been happening in their small town, many of them would defend him and his family's actions. It was for the good of the town, she could almost hear them say. They were just doing what they thought was best. She had only been back in town a few days, but Jaime already felt like she had overstayed her welcome.

The ride back to Flynn's house was filled with an uncomfortable silence. Each of them lost in the thought that they had just decided they needed to kill a man. If they did, in fact, go through with it, and kill Chris, would they be any better than him? This thought came to Jaime's mind, and her immediate reaction was that his death would mean others would live. That in the end, it would help generations of people. She then realized that this thought probably crossed every person's mind whose name was on the piece of paper in her pocket. Her stomach lurched at the thought, and she reached her right arm out to roll down her window.

The cool air was a relief when it first hit her in the face. She closed her eyes and let the air rush over her like a cold shower. She might have fallen asleep if not for Flynn crying out in alarm, and slamming on the brakes.

Her eyes flew open, and she was thrown forward against her seatbelt which locked in place. She could already feel a bruise forming on her right collar bone where the belt had grabbed her.

"The fuck?" She cried out. Her eyes scanned the road for a dog or some other animal. That was when she saw it, and her heart leapt into her throat.

Standing in the middle of the road, only about five yards away, illuminated by the headlights was the thing that had haunted Jaime's dreams for the last fifteen years.

"Holy shit! Holy shit!" Came the shout from the backseat. "It's fucking real! It's really fucking real!"

Jaime and Flynn both suppressed the urge to tell Jared to shut the hell up as they focused all their attention on the being that was standing in front of them. In all of Jaime's nightmares, the demon never seemed to have a real body, just a black mass. Seeing it again after all these years, Jaime realized that was because that's all it really was. It mostly reminded her of the Ghost of Christmas Future in Charles Dickens' *A Christmas Carol.* It appeared to be wearing a black robe of sorts, two distinct arm sleeves, but no arms or hands that Jaime could see. A hood of some sort covered its face, something else that Jaime had never seen. She wasn't even positive that it had a face and not just a black hole. The antlers, though, they were exactly as Jaime remembered. Giant, bone white, looming sculptures they were. They were so high off the demon's head, Jaime still wasn't sure how they never got caught on low hanging branches.

"What the fuck happened?" Jaime asked Flynn. "Did it dart out in front of you?"

"No," he answered with his breath coming out in short gasps. "I looked up, and it was just there. Like it had been waiting for us the entire time."

The words inside the Jeep seemed to snap the demon out of the trance it appeared to be in. It turned away from them, and made its way into the woods on the right side of the road where it disappeared into the trees. It glided, not walked, just as Jaime remembered.

As soon as it entered the trees, Flynn edged the Jeep forward to where the demon had stood just moments before. Jaime strained her eyes against the dark, searching for a flash of the white antlers in the sea of trees, knowing all too well that it was gone.

Jared was still muttering nonsense words and sentences from the back seat. He was really starting to get on her nerves. Had he been the one who ran into this thing fifteen years ago, Jaime knew without a doubt, he would have crumbled and broken down in the middle of that field. Thankfully, Flynn turned around in his seat and told Jared to get a hold of himself. Panicking was only going to make things worse. After a few seconds of deep breaths and shaky exhales, he finally managed to string together a coherent thought.

"If I survive this night," he began. "I swear I will spend the rest of my life making it up to you for what I said and did to you fifteen years ago, Jaime."

"Let's work on the first half of that promise, and then once this thing is gone, we'll work out the details of the second half." Jaime replied, trying to sound funny.

"Let's just get home, and work out a plan there," Flynn insisted, wanting to put as much distance between them and the demon as possible for the moment.

"No," Jaime commanded. "We can't go anywhere near home right now. The only reason that thing appeared here tonight was because it was waiting for us."

"Do you think Chris knows what I told you guys? That I was in the Jeep?" Jared was now completely terrified, and Jaime couldn't blame him.

"I have no idea, but my guess is no. He told you everything about his family. We had a lot of it figured out, but you filled in the blanks that we needed. I think if he knew you had betrayed his trust, he would've sent that thing after you, and us, hours ago."

Hearing this, Jared put his head in his hands and forced himself to keep his emotions under control. This wasn't the time or place for him to have a breakdown.

For a second, Jaime felt bad for him, but only for a second. Then she remembered he sold out his own wife to this thing because she wasn't easy to control anymore. Amber was finally realizing that she had made a mistake marrying him, and he couldn't handle it. Jared was scared she was going to leave him, so he got someone else to get rid of her before she could leave on her own. The disgust he had always filled her with came rushing back, but she forced herself to push it down. Once this was all over, she could take out her rage on him.

"If we can't go home, where do we go?" Flynn asked. His eyes were constantly scanning the sides of the road. He didn't want this thing getting the jump on them again. Although, he thought, if this thing wanted to surprise them, there probably wasn't much they could do to prevent it.

Jaime thought hard for a minute. Her mind raced, but she forced it to quiet so she could think what the next move should be. On a whim, she turned around and asked Jared a question.

"Where does Chris live? He lives in town, right?"

Jared nodded.

"He's lived in the same house since the three of us were in high school. He lives over on Corner Ave."

Here Jared paused to emit a small watery chuckle.

"He actually lives behind the street from where Amber's parents live. The house Amber grew up in."

Jaime felt the blood drain from her face upon hearing this. She could see Flynn's knuckles grip the wheel even tighter, and he straightened in his seat.

"Excuse me?" Flynn managed to squeak out.

"Yeah," Jared continued, completely unaware of what he had just helped them realize. "I've been over there a bunch of times for spaghetti dinners and parties. It's actually where Amber and I first got to really talking at a cookout after we were already out of high school."

"That bastard saw me come out of that house that night," Jaime growled. "He probably saw me every time I snuck out of Amber's window. That night though, he decided that he wanted to have some fun, so he sent his pet after me. He never expected me to get away. It would have been the mystery of the century as to where I disappeared to. My parents would have believed I was taken right out of my bedroom that night, unless Amber had come forward. And she never would've if it meant dealing with the aftermath of her parents. Nope, my picture would've been on all the TV stations, and telephone poles, and *60 Minutes* would've done a special on the ten-year anniversary of my disappearance, and he would have been the only person who ever knew the truth."

She finished, and then pressed her knuckles against her lips, in an effort to stop them from trembling. Her vision began to blur from tears until she forced them back. She couldn't afford to lose control just yet.

"We need to get to that bastard's house," she gritted out. "Before anyone else gets hurt."

With a nod, Flynn made a quick U-turn and pressed his foot down hard on the gas pedal.

Thankfully, the cops had better things to be doing that night than looking for speeding vehicles on back roads, and they arrived at Chris' house in record time. Flynn opted to park the Jeep in the field Jaime had run through fifteen years prior, instead of on the street near the other houses. They didn't want to spook Chris, at least not yet, and didn't want to draw any unwanted attention. After a short, tension-filled walk they arrived at Chris' house. His truck was parked in the driveway, and the lights were on downstairs. They hung back in the bushes across the street for a moment, trying to decide how they wanted to proceed.

But before they could come to a group resolution, Jared made the decision for them all.

"You two hang around out here," he blurted out. "I'm going in there. He still doesn't know that I went to you guys. Let's use that to our advantage."

And just like that, he stalked towards the front door before either one of them could pull him back. It wasn't a great plan, but Jaime had to admit it was really the only one that made sense. If her and Flynn showed up on the doorstep, Chris would immediately know something was up and he would probably lash out. Jared could at least get through the door without triggering any alarms in Chris' head.

"This is probably the first time ever that he's actually made a legitimate leadership decision, and put others ahead of himself," Flynn whispered. "I just don't know if it was a good one."

They watched as Jared rung the bell, and then stepped back from the door. A few seconds later, the door opened and Chris greeted him like an old friend. They hung outside for a second, and then Chris held out his arm, welcoming Jared inside.

"One of us should probably circle around back, make sure nobody tries to make a break for it," Jaime murmured as they came out from behind the bushes.

"You stay here," Flynn insisted. "I'll sneak around and see if I can hear them say anything through a window. I still have no idea what I'm going to do if Chris comes barreling out the back door."

"Try to force him towards the woods and away from any other houses. We don't need anyone else getting hurt tonight."

With a nod, he was gone. For someone as big as Flynn, it was impressive to watch him slink around in the dark. He reminded Jaime of some kind of jungle cat stalking its prey. He disappeared out of view, and Jaime felt her stomach tighten. She knew Flynn could take care of himself, but it still didn't make her feel any better about splitting up. Suddenly, she knew exactly how Scooby-Doo and Shaggy felt whenever the gang split up to look for clues.

From her position in the bushes, she couldn't see much except for the front window. Every now and then, one of the guys inside would pass in front of it, but she couldn't tell if they were talking, arguing, or dancing. She felt useless just sitting there in the bushes, hiding, but she knew that they needed to do this right.

Each minute that passed felt like an hour crouched down behind the bushes. By now Jaime was convinced she'd never be able to stand again after kneeling in the wet grass for so long. Her toes had long gone numb, and her fingers were on their way to joining them when she heard a commotion coming from the house. There was the sound of what Jaime could only describe as a door being kicked in, and then she heard Flynn call her name. She was up on her feet immediately, and although she could feel neither her feet or knees, she was hauling ass to get to the backyard.

Twenty-One

The door opened and Jared forced himself to smile. He couldn't afford to look scared right now.

"Well, this is a surprise!" Chris exclaimed, throwing his arms open as if for a hug when he found his old friend standing behind his front door. "Come on in! You want a beer?"

"No thanks, I'm good for now," Jared answered, trying to sound like he wanted to be there. "I was out walking, going over some things in my head for the game Friday, and I figured I'd just stop in and run some of them by you. I'm a little concerned with how Rogers hasn't been progressing as much as we would have liked the last couple weeks of practice."

"Oh man," Chris moaned popping open a beer can. Hearing the tell-tale beer can opening sound, Jared almost asked for one himself. He knew though, that he needed a clear head. "Tell me about it. That kid had the starting job locked up coming into the season. But it seems like the only thing he did all summer was eat pizza and play videogames. He can barely run the wind sprints at the end of practice, let alone the offense with that fat ass. I'm thinking we're going to have to sit him down, and tell him he needs to lose fifteen pounds before we give him the keys to the car, so to speak."

Any other time, and talk like this would have had Jared rolling with laughter. But now, it made him uncomfortable. How had he never seen what kind of guy Chris was before? Or maybe he had, and just chose to ignore it. He forced out a laugh anyway, so that Chris wouldn't think something was wrong. Apparently, the laugh wasn't as convincing as he thought, because Chris still shot him a funny look.

"You okay, man? You seem a little off tonight."

"Yeah, I'm just tired. A lot been going on these last couple weeks."

"Well, at least you don't have that bitch at home anymore. She's finally where she belongs."

As if to drive this point home, he finished the rest of his beer in three big gulps, and then crushed the can in his hand.

Jared felt his hands clench into fists, and his anger rise up inside him. He couldn't believe he had let this guy talk him into sacrificing his wife to his family's pet.

"Yeah, it's great, man. I can finally leave my pants on the floor instead of having to put them in the laundry basket."

He tried to keep his voice light, and a smirk on his face. He wanted Chris to believe that he was loving his new lifestyle. In reality, he had been sleeping on the couch instead of in the bedroom. Ever since the night after Amber's disappearance, Jared had been having vivid and terrifying nightmares. In his latest one, he found himself out on the high school's football field all alone under the blinding stadium lights. He's wearing his football uniform from high school with his helmet tucked under his left arm. Suddenly, the turf opens up and begin to suck him in. First his cleats disappear, then his shins, and finally his knees. No matter how hard he struggles the turf grips him tight. Out of nowhere, the lights click off and he's left in the dark, but only for a few seconds. When the lights come back on, Amber is standing in front of him, but it's not the Amber he remembers. The left side of her head is caved in from a heavy blow, and her left eye is swollen with blood, ready to burst at any moment. Her entire head now sits at a crooked angle with its muscles straining against the skin. She's wearing the yellow sweater he got her for her birthday the previous year, but it's now maroon with blood. She limps closer without a word. Jared opens his mouth to scream that he's sorry, that he wishes he could take back everything that has happened, nothing comes out. He feels a warm sensation creep down his legs and realizes he's wet his pants. Just as Amber leans her twisted, purple face down to meet his, Jared screams himself awake. Once his breathing returned to normal, and he managed to get the living room lamp on, he discovers that not only did he wet himself in his dream, but also in real life.

"Hell yeah," Chris responded as he cracked open another can. "Bachelor's life is the way to live. Can't beat that shit. Nobody bitchin' at you to clean the kitchen, or to take the trash out, or any of that shit."

He paused here and took a long gulp of his beer. After, he swiped the back of his hand across his mouth to catch the liquid that had escaped his lips, then he continued.

"Speaking of that. I've been meaning to talk to you about something. About the future of my family's work."

Jared couldn't hide the puzzled look on his face when Chris said this. What could he possibly need to talk to him about?

"The Settlement has been passed down in my family since the founding of this town. Whenever the current holder of the Settlement starts getting older, or sick, they make the decision as to who in the family should take over the helm."

Jared's heart was pounding in his chest. He was pretty sure he knew where this was going, and he wanted nothing to do with it.

"As you know, I don't have any wife or children, and I was an only child. I don't have any intention of getting married or having kids anytime soon. I don't have any other family, so in order to keep the family tradition alive, I'm going to need to find someone I trust to take it over when I'm gone. Someone who I know will do whatever it takes to protect this town and its people. I want you to be that person for me, man."

Jared's head was spinning. Once upon a time, the idea of being in control of an all-powerful being would have filled him with exhilaration. He would have killed for the chance to do something like that in high school. But now, knowing what he knew about the disappearances that the families of the town had suffered through, after offering his own wife up as one of the sacrifices, well, he thought he'd rather kill himself than sign his name on that piece of paper.

"Hey man, that's great and all. Really, thanks for wanting me to do that, but I don't think I have the stomach for it."

"I don't think you understand," came the cold response. "You know too much to not be the next in line. You need to take this secret to the grave with you. The Settlement needs a holder, and the town needs a protector. The only other person alive who has seen the demon is that bitch you graduated with, and no one has ever believed anything she said about that night, except that basketball player who always followed her around like a lost puppy. Hopefully, now that that candlelight vigil for Amber is over with, she'll be leaving town soon and we won't have to worry about her for at least another fifteen years. Or –."

Chris licked his lips and turned an icy stare to Jared. "Or we could make sure we don't have to worry about her and that puppy permanently."

Jared knew that Chris was talking about sending the demon after them, and he unfortunately couldn't hide the grimace that crossed his face. Chris noticed the change, and asked him about it.

"You actually feeling sorry for those losers?" Chris spat in disgust.

Jared tried to recover as best he could, hiding his concern for Jaime and Flynn by saying it would be in their own best interests.

"Two other people going missing so close to Amber going missing? Two people who knew Amber. You don't think that might bring about a bigger investigation? I think we need to lay low for the time being."

Chris looked at him after he had finished. His eyes narrowed, and they held Jared's, daring him to look away. To Jared, it felt like he was trying to read his mind, to see how he actually felt about the idea of killing Jaime and Flynn.

"You sure you're okay? You've been acting a little weird since you showed up, but ever since I mentioned that you were going to be taking over the Settlement one day, you've been completely off. The Jared I've known for most of my adult life would be psyched about this. But you're not. Why? Hell, a couple days ago, you were pumped that you didn't have a wife anymore, but now you look like you want to burst into tears whenever you hear her name. When did you become such a pansy all of a sudden? Huh?"

His tone had shifted from mostly joking to fury in the blink of an eye. He was puffing his chest out, to make himself look bigger like he had done his entire life on the football field when he needed to intimidate young and inexperienced players into thinking they were shit. He had always paired it with a cocky grin on his face, daring the player, and now Jared, to stand up to him, knowing full well that they never would. Jared was starting to see how much of a bully this guy had always been. He probably came from a long line of bullies who used fear and embarrassment to get what they wanted.

Not anymore, Jared thought. He had played his own part in bullying people in high school, and he knew he could never take that back. And now was his chance to help make things right in the here and now.

"You're not going to get away with this any longer," Jared growled out. His hands had clenched into fists again, and he could feel his blood pumping through his veins. Chris' cocky grin fell away from his face immediately seeing that Jared wasn't going to back down.

"This thing your family started, it's not a protector. It's a disease. It's a parasite that shows up and eats people, good people! This ends now, no more!"

"Who do you suppose is going to stop this? You? Please, you couldn't even read the blitz in high school. You expect me to believe you came up with a plan all by your lonesome?"

At this, Jared's eyes flicked away from Chris' stare for half a second. But it was the final piece of the puzzle Chris needed. Chris' eyes widened ever so slightly before narrowing to slits. His nostrils flared, and Jared could hear him grind his teeth together.

"That's why you don't want me to go after the bitch and the puppy. You're working with those fuckers. You son of a bitch."

Before Jared could deny or confirm, Chris launched himself at Jared's chest and slammed him against the refrigerator. They hit so hard that Jared felt the fridge rise up on its back two feet and come crashing back down on the floor.

"You ungrateful little shit! I trusted you!" Chris screamed as he grabbed Jared by the shirt and slammed his head back against the fridge over and over.

Jared knew he had to get free or else he'd be unconscious in a matter of minutes, and then Jaime and Flynn would really be in deep shit. With all the strength he could muster, he pushed himself away from the fridge and used his momentum to force Chris off himself. As Chris stumbled back, Jared used these few seconds to glance around the kitchen for any kind of weapon he could grab. On the counter, he spotted a utility knife sitting next to some old beer cartons that Chris had been using to cut them up. He immediately closed his fist around it, and then saw a frying pan on the stove forgotten from last night's grilled cheese sandwiches. Thinking this might be a better option for the moment, he grabbed the handle and swung as hard as he could where Chris was. Chris managed to get his arms up before the frying pan connected, but Jared still landed a solid blow. There was a loud crack, and Chris screamed. Not wanting to give him any chance of recovery, Jared pulled the frying pan back and swung again. This time, however, Chris was expecting it and was able to knock the impromptu weapon aside before he grabbed ahold of Jared.

They stumbled around for a few seconds, locked together like two rams fighting for dominance. Both were injured enough to warrant medical attention. Chris was cradling a broken radius and ulna in his left arm from where he had been hit with the frying pan. Jared could feel something sticky trailing down the back of his neck, and didn't need to reach his hand back to know the fridge had done more damage to him than he originally thought. Jared broke free for a moment, just long enough to take a few deep breaths, but then Chris reared back and charged like a stampeding rhino. He plowed into Jared, who had the wind knocked out of him, and they both plowed into the back door. The wooden frame broke free and spilled them out into the backyard where Flynn was waiting.

The two men rolled once, twice and then came to a stop lying about two yards away from one another.

"Hey!" Flynn called out, rushing over from where he was hidden behind one of the bushes in the backyard. "Jaime! Get back here!"

But before he could get to the two men sprawled out in the yard, Chris was up on his feet hightailing it towards the woods where he disappeared amongst the trees for the time being.

Twenty-Two

Jaime rounded the corner of the house, and skidded to a halt when she saw Flynn helping Jared up off the ground.

"What the hell happened?" she called. "Where's Chris?"

"He took off into the woods after he threw Jared through the backdoor," Flynn responded after setting Jared on his feet again. His shirt had been ripped along the collar where Chris had grabbed him. There appeared to be blood dripping down the side of his head, and even in the dark, Jaime could see a bruise already forming on his right temple.

"He knows," Jared moaned. He was holding his right arm tight against his stomach and grimacing in pain. "He knows that I went to you guys tonight. He got it out of me. He would've killed me if I hadn't gotten my hands on something to defend myself. I was able to nail him pretty good with a frying pan he had laying on the counter, and I was able to grab this right before he tackled me through the door,"

He held up the four-inch utility knife he had swiped from the counter.

"It's not much, but it was the only thing I could get my hands on."

"It's better than what we showed up here with," Jaime shrugged. "Are you going to be okay to go after him?"

Jared nodded, but they all could see how much pain he was in.

"He's not going to get away with this any longer. Let's go."

It was rough going at first. Without the light of the moon, which had gone behind the clouds for the moment, it was hard to navigate over roots and under tree branches that seemed to stretch out in front of them like a witch's fingernails. They had no idea if they were even going in the right direction, or if Chris had circled back and was now creeping up on them. All they could do was press forward, and keep their ears and eyes open for a sneak attack.

Jared relayed the story of what happened inside Chris' home as they trudged through the underbrush. His breathing was becoming increasingly labored, and Jaime was beginning to worry he was seriously injured.

"He's probably going to send the demon after all three of us," Jared added at the end of his tale.

"Do you think he'd take that chance? He has to know how much attention three missing persons would bring about." Flynn asked as he held back a low hanging branch so the other two could safely pass.

"He's getting desperate," Jared wheezed. "He knows if he doesn't do something, this whole thing is going to come crashing down on him. He's going to make a stand, tonight."

The trio stumbled along for several minutes unsure of where they were or where they were going. Both Jaime and Flynn had spent a considerable amount of time in the woods around town growing up, but they had never been in these parts, and therefore had no idea what the terrain was like, or even what was in the area. Which is why they were all so surprised to find themselves come into a small clearing.

The clearing was about twenty feet wide all around, and it was in the shape of a circle. The ground was all dirt. There was no sign of grass, and it appeared that there hadn't been grass in this spot for a long time. The only thing located in the clearing was a large rock situated in what looked like the dead center.

The three carefully made their way through the clearing, scanning the perimeter constantly, trying to anticipate an attack if one was coming. As they grew closer to the rock and the center of the clearing, they noticed there was something chiseled into the rock. The three silently drew forward and began to examine what had been carved into the surface of the stone. They discovered it was a symbol of sorts. A circle about five inches in diameter was perfectly etched into the rock. Inside the top half of the circle was a simple drawing of an eye, and beneath that eye in the bottom of the circle appeared to be flames.

"Hey, hang on a sec," Jared said patting the pockets of his jeans. He pulled out his cellphone and quickly turned on his flashlight app. "Looks like it got a little dinged up in the fight, but at least this still works."

With the light, the three leaned in closer to get a better look at the symbol.

"Shit. That's the crest I've seen at Chris' house, with that family name above it." Jared moaned.

Underneath the symbol, and all over the rock, were more carvings. Some they could tell were older than they were, and were hard to read. Others were fresher and could still be deciphered after a little squinting. Flynn squatted down in front of the rock and leaned in close trying to see what he could make out.

"Everything else looks like just a bunch of scribbles," Flynn explained. "They all look – ." He broke off mid-sentence after something caught his attention. He leaned in closer, and then suddenly pulled his head back as if he had been burned. He twisted around to look at his two compatriots, and shot them a look full of fear.

"You guys gotta see this. This is how he's been doing it. How he's able to pick and choose when he wants to."

Jaime and Jared fell to their knees on either side of Flynn, the light from Jared's phone shook as he struggled to keep it steady. Their eyes scanned the scribbles, searching for anything legible. Finally, both sets of eyes landed on the same name, AMBER MCCLOSKEY, and they let out two simultaneous gasps.

"I'm gonna go out on a limb here," Flynn continued. "I'm thinking this is where the original deal went down, and the Settlement was signed."

"Look at all these names. All these people over the years the Gallagher's have put the hit out on," Jaime groaned.

Her eyes then landed on something that made the world spin underneath her. She felt like she was falling so she reached out and clutched the rock. Her vision blurred and for a second she thought she might faint. Not as clear as Amber's name, a little worn from the last fifteen years, but there it was, JAMIE STRAIT.

Flynn and Jared both had reached out to steady her when she nearly pitched forward. Their eyes then fell upon what she had seen, and they both let out cries of rage and fear.

"He spelled it wrong," she whispered almost to herself. "The bastard spelled my name wrong. That's why I was able to get away that night. It couldn't take me, because the name wasn't right."

"This is way bigger than I thought," Jared sputtered. "How many people has he made disappear over the years? How many families don't know what happened to their loved ones?" He looked back down at Amber's name, the one he himself had helped to chisel on this rock.

Maybe not physically, but he was responsible for its existence. He suddenly couldn't take it anymore. He jumped to his feet, stumbled a few yards away, and vomited on the ground.

Jaime and Flynn let him get it out of his system and pull himself together.

"You got a plan yet?" Flynn asked his best friend as his eyes continuously scanned the tree line for any sign of Chris and the demon.

"Sort of, but you're not going to like it."

"At this point, I'm open to just about anything."

He listened as Jaime explained what was running through her head. His eyes widened as she talked, and once she was done he reacted about how she expected.

"When I said just about anything, I wasn't talking about that!"

"I'll do it," came a shaky, tearful voice from behind them.

They turned around to face Jared as he made his way back over to where they were standing at the rock. His face was so pale, Jaime was sure he was seconds away from fainting.

"I heard your plan. It's the only play we have right now if we want to draw Chris out. I'm partially responsible for this mess, so it only makes sense that I should be the one to help make things right."

"You should know I have no idea what we're going to do even if everything goes as planned," Jaime explained to Jared. She knew she didn't owe this guy anything, but she still felt obligated to let him know what he was getting himself into.

"I know. Let's worry about one thing at a time, shall we?"

Twenty-Three

"You ready?" Flynn asked the guy who he had spent most of his life hating. He still couldn't believe that he was making what could be their final stand with this asshat. Although, now, Flynn thought, this guy had probably moved up a notch from asshat, especially after agreeing to Jaime's plan.

"Hell no," came the answer. "But let's do it before I change my mind."

"Little late for that," Flynn mumbled under his breath as Jared moved away from the rock.

"Chris! Hey, Chris!" Jared screamed. "We know you're out here somewhere! We want to talk! You were right! Come on, man! I promise no tricks! We just want to work everything out!"

The dice had been rolled, and now it was time to wait. They were confident that Chris was in the area somewhere. They hoped against all hope that he hadn't been close enough to hear them and their plain. They all stayed extremely still, listening for any rustling that might have been Chris. Jared stood in the center of the clearing, his left hand cupped around his mouth, his entire right arm clutched tightly against his side. Flynn wasn't far from him, head cocked and ears straining for any sound. His mouth was drawn into a tight line, and his hands had already curled into fists. Next to him stood Jaime. Her eyes darted from tree to tree searching for any kind of movement. She shifted her weight from foot to foot, ready to jump into fight mode, or if things went to shit in a hurry, flight mode.

Just when they thought he wasn't going to show; that he had already made his escape to somewhere else in town, they heard leaves crunching coming from the opposite side of the clearing they had entered from. Jaime tensed for a moment, her mind travelling back to fifteen years ago. Suddenly sure that the demon would step out of the trees instead of Chris. The crunching got closer and louder, until finally Chris did stumble out of the trees. He was sweating profusely and breathing heavily It was clear that he had been injured in his fight with Jared. His face was twisted in anger and pain, and obviously was skeptical about Jared's claims of 'no tricks'. His eyes never wandered off Jared.

"You wanna talk," Chris called as he came to a stop far enough away from them so he could spot an ambush. "Talk. I'm listening."

Jared raised his left hand to show he meant no harm, as his right arm hung uselessly against his side. Flynn and Jaime did the same with both of their hands, but Chris wasn't interested in them, at least not for the moment.

"Look man," he began slowly. "We know you and your family had the best of intentions for the town, but this has gone too far. I never should have agreed to let you help with Amber. I didn't know what you had in mind, but that still doesn't clear me of my part in this. This needs to stop."

Chris immediately went on the aggressive. He took two giant steps forward towards the trio and then stopped again.

"This town would be in ruins if it wasn't for my family!" he bawled. "It's my destiny to protect this town! Nobody else in this bumfuck town has the balls to do what I've done!"

Jared turned his head slightly to glance at Flynn for a second, looking for some encouragement. Flynn nodded, looked down at

Jaime, and then twirled his left hand in a circle, the universal signal for keep it going.

"I get that," Jared called back. "Hey, man. I totally get it. We've had some great years here, and I'm guessing we owe a lot of that to you and your family. And hey, you're pissed that people will never know the truth. You and your family deserve a lot of credit and recognition, but you're never going to get that, are you? You'll have to live in anonymity forever, and in your mind, that's a fate worse than death."

Chris stood unblinking, mulling over Jared's words. His breathing was growing more labored by the minute, and his left arm was visibly swollen and beginning to discolor. Finally, he started laughing.

"Jared," he began. It came out soundly almost comforting. "Come with me. I can show and teach you things you can't even imagine.

Let me teach you about what my family has done for this town. We're not monsters. We're protectors, guardians. But now, my family is gone and so is yours. I need someone to take over for me when I get too old, and I want that person to be you."

Jared stood looking at Chris unsure of what to say next, when he heard Jaime speak up from behind him.

"You're no protector." Jaime's voice was clear, and despite the weight of the next words, never wavered. "You're a killer, plain and simple. You tried to kill me fifteen years ago, which didn't go as planned."

Chris' eyes narrowed and his lips curled as his attention was now drawn to Jaime.

"You always treated me like shit in class, and I could never figure out why. Always just figured you hated girls, but now I know that it's because I was the one who got away. All because you couldn't spell my fucking name right. Hopefully, we're a little better with spelling than you were."

At first, Chris took a step towards them as if ready to attack. He hated being mocked, especially by a little gay bitch. And then he realized what it was that Jaime had said. The anger melted away from his face and in its place, was humor.

"You really think that writing my name on that rock will put me in the path of destruction?" he laughed. "You're dumber than you look if that's the case."

"Good thing we're not dumb then," Flynn quipped as Jared reached into his pocket. When he pulled out his hand he was holding the rolled-up Settlement. He held it out so that Chris could see what it was.

"You're bluffing!" he screamed when he realized what it was. "There's no fucking way you could have gotten your hands on that! I changed the lock myself!"

"And used your own football jersey numbers as the combination. Now who's dumber than they look?" Jaime goaded.

"That doesn't change anything! Just because you have that, and wrote my name on the rock doesn't mean anything! My name is the one on the Settlement, so I'm still the one in charge!"

Slowly, Jared raised his injured right arm away from his side to reveal his hand. It was covered in blood that had dripped down from a cut on his index finger. He then unrolled the paper and held it out so that the writing faced Chris. Now that the moon had since reappeared from behind the clouds, he had no problem seeing the new writing at the bottom of the paper.

Suddenly, Jaime's ears perked up. Ever so softly, there were footsteps crunching their way towards them. She didn't think any of the others could hear them, and for a second she thought she was simply imaging them until the sound began to grow louder as the steps grew closer to the clearing. Jaime could feel her heartbeat begin to rise, but she thought it was in anticipation rather than fear this time.

Chris' eyes drifted from the Settlement back to Jared's, then to Flynn's, and finally to Jaime's. They expected to see fear, anger even, but what they saw instead was excitement.

"I knew you could do it!" he exclaimed to Jared. "I knew you had the balls to become what I had become! To make the hard decisions, and be the one to watch over this town!"

The crunching sound was unavoidable now. It was coming from directly behind Chris, but nothing but the vast, dark emptiness of the woods could be seen.

"You really are a psychopath," Jaime spat with disgust. "You've been waiting for this day since you first took over the Settlement. You've always wanted to be one of your so-called sacrifices."

"I admit, I hadn't planned on this day happening for many years to come, but I knew that this would be how I would go out. I knew it from the day I signed the Settlement with my father. It's how he went out, how my grandfather went out, how several other members of my family went out. I welcome my fate with open arms."

The trees where the crunching was coming from began to sway and rustle. In addition to the crunching the air grew thick and humid. In the distance, above the trees a lightning bolt streaked across the sky. Suddenly, seemingly out of thin air, a pair of antlers erupted from the trees. The demon stood on the edge of the clearing for a moment, seeming to pause and size up its prey.

Jaime didn't think she would ever get used to seeing the demon, although she prayed to every deity she could think of that this was the last time she would ever see the damn thing. She was pretty confident that this would work, but she wasn't going to be satisfied until Chris was gone. They had no idea how they were going to get Jared out of the Settlement, but he had agreed they could figure it out later. Chris was a walking time bomb at the reins of this thing.

The demon paused briefly before it lurched forward, gliding across the ground effortlessly. Chris closed his eyes in ecstasy and tilted his face up towards the moon which for a moment was awash in light. Tears streamed down on his face, but the corners of his mouth were drawn upward. His face, which was utterly peaceful, content with his fate, was more haunting to Jaime than the demon itself. He was like a death row inmate on his way to Ole' Sparky. He had made his peace with the world, with everything he had done, and was ready for whatever came next.

Closer and closer the demon got, silent as the grave. It never made a single sound as it approached the group. Finally, it came to a stop directly behind Chris. If it breathed, Jaime was sure Chris could feel its breath on the back of his neck. Jaime remembered it being tall, but she never could have guessed how gigantic it actually was. It stood at least two heads taller than Chris, and even Flynn had to tilt his head back slightly to look up at it. Once Chris felt its presence, he turned slowly to face it. He looked up into its black hole of a face with what could only be described as awe, and spoke.

"I will give my breath for this town, so that the future may thrive."

With speed faster than anything they had ever seen before, the demon reached up and grasped Chris by the shoulders. Two hands, if that's what they were, extended from the sleeves of the demon's robe. They consisted of three, gray, scaly fingers. At the tip of each finger was a three-inch, black claw that would have looked at home in one of the *Jurassic Park* films. Jaime immediately thought of the first one, where the velociraptor opens the door while hunting the two kids. They could see Chris wince as the claws dug into him.

They remained this way for a few seconds longer. Everyone held their breath for the inevitable. Jaime expected the actual sacrificial part to be loud and violent, and she was preparing herself for an explosion of sorts.

The demon held Chris firmly in its grasp. Any sudden movement by Chris, and his shoulders would have been cut to ribbons. But he stayed where he was, he was clearly enjoying all the attention. Then, out of nowhere, smoke began to rise from Chris, just small wisps at first. It didn't dissipate right away like normal smoke would. It twirled out of his legs, arms, and his head and circled his body in a sort of dance.

Seconds passed and more and more smoke appeared and danced. As more smoke appeared, Chris became less himself, more see through. His skin became transparent and one could see every vein and artery coursing through his body. Soon they disappeared and his muscles and tendons came into view. More smoke and more smoke oozed out until it was so thick that it hid what was left of Chris' body.

Jaime hoped it hurt like hell.

Twenty-Four

After only about a minute, Chris' entire corporeal form was now completely smoke. But still it didn't move like normal campfire smoke. It stayed right where the demon wanted it. Finally, after letting it dance in front of it, the demon tilted its faceless head backwards and the smoke lifted up towards it. The smoke poured into the hole where a face should have been, but wasn't. When the smoke was gone, and the demon sated for the moment, it tilted its head back down again and looked at the remaining three bodies standing in the clearing.

We're next for sure, Jaime thought. Their plan worked with Chris, but it wants more. Jared will be spared, but Flynn and I are goners. It needs more sacrifices.

Just when Jaime thought her pounding heart would leap up out of her throat, the demon made an about face, and headed back the way it had originally come out of the trees. It hit the tree line and they could hear the leaves crunch once more. The crunching ceased after a moment and the bone white antlers disappeared into thin air. It never indicated it would be back to finish the job. Its work was done for the night. That was the moment Jaime realized that the demon really wasn't the bad guy. It never took more than it absolutely needed. Like so many other situations in life, the creature wasn't the monster in this scenario. That honor went to the humans, as usual.

Once they could no longer hear the crunching of the leaves anymore, Jared turned and held the Settlement out to Jaime.

"I don't think I want to hold this anymore," Jared moaned and his face was drained of color. "It makes me feel sick just to look at it."

Jaime nodded, took hold of it, ignored the goosebumps that erupted on her arms, and rolled it back up. She shoved it into the pocket of her jeans and tried to push it to the back of her mind. She wasn't really a big fan of holding onto it right now, but she still wasn't sure if they would need it down the road.

It took them almost twenty minutes to make their way through the woods and back to the Jeep. They paused momentarily in Chris' backyard to look at the door which had been kicked outward. Flynn decided to close it as best he could, so it wouldn't draw too much attention right away. Once Chris didn't show up for school, someone would come looking and find the mess. Hopefully they'd have a plan by then. One look at the kitchen inside and the police would know a struggle had happened. They decided they'd cross that bridge when they came to it.

"Why don't you just crash at my place tonight?" Flynn offered to Jared as he turned the key in the ignition. They had made their way back to the Jeep, and all but collapsed into their seats.

"We can keep an eye on that head of yours." Jaime added as she turned in the passenger seat to look back at Jared. He was sitting up, to his credit, staring out the window into the bleak night seemingly lost in thought. Jaime tilted her head and studied him for a moment. Even in the dark Jeep, she could see how much these events had aged him. His eyes which had always held a mischievous glint, now looked dull and sunken in. Jaime only now realized how thin Jared looked. The skin on his face appeared taunt, stretched tight over his skull, giving him a skeletal appearance.

"Hey." Jaime called to Jared softly which caused him to startle. "You still with us?"

"I – uh, yeah." Jared said as he shook his head which caused him to wince. "Sorry. Mind's all over the place right now. Thanks for the offer, but I think I need to go to my place tonight, get my head right again."

Flynn nodded as he glanced into the rearview mirror to look at Jared.

"Okay. We'll come over and pick you up around noon, after a few hours of sleep. Guess we all need to get our stories straight for when word of Chris' disappearance hits the streets."

Moments later Flynn pulled up to Jared's house, cut the headlights, and threw the Jeep into park. It took Jared almost an entire minute to get himself out of the backseat and onto the sidewalk. His arm had gone mostly numb, every step sent a bolt of pain through his head, and he was sore basically everywhere. During the car ride he had discovered one of his teeth had been knocked loose, and his tongue kept nudging it back and forth. Once he was out and steadied himself on his shaky legs, Jaime rolled her window down to address him.

"It took a lot of guts to do what you did tonight. I'm not sure I could have put my name down on that paper like you did. I know you and I don't have the greatest history but, thanks for all your help tonight."

Jared looked down at his feet after hearing this, suddenly feeling very shy.

"No," he responded. "No, it took a lot of guts for you fifteen years ago to walk into school every day knowing that you were going to get laughed at and mocked. It took a lot of guts for you to come back to this fucking town to face something only you knew about. To come back to a place that turned its back on you, to help that place, to help people who ridiculed you. Well, I'm not sure I could have done that. You're a better person than I ever was, both of you, than I ever will be. So, really the thanks goes to you guys."

They watched him limp up the front walk, and then disappear behind his front door. Jaime leaned back in the passenger's seat and closed her eyes as Jared's words rang in her ears. Never in million years did she ever think she'd hear Jared utter those words, what resembled an apology. She felt tears tickle the back of her eyelids, and she forced them down. She wasn't worried about crying in front of Flynn; she had done that enough over the years. It was just that Jaime knew that there was more work to be done, and that she couldn't afford to breakdown just yet.

"You okay?" Flynn prodded gently. "It's been a rough night."

"Yeah," she rasped. "Let's go home, get some sleep. We'll figure the rest of this out in the morning."

Twenty-Five

Despite having spent a good portion of the night out saving the town, both Jaime and Flynn were awake by seven A.M. sitting at the kitchen table drinking coffee. Neither of them had slept particularly well. Both couldn't seem to get comfortable no matter how much they tossed and turned.

"I thought things would be better after we got rid of Chris," Flynn said rubbing a hand over his face. "But I think things are now more complicated than ever."

Jaime opened her mouth to reply, her hands cupped around her mug desperate to absorb its warmth when she stopped. She cocked her head to the side and looked off as if deep in thought.

"You hear that?" she asked.

Flynn strained his ears, listening hard for whatever it was that had gotten Jaime's attention. Finally, his face changed from that of a confused puppy dog to one of horror.

"Sirens."

"Get dressed," Flynn jumped up out of his seat leaving their coffee mugs to grow cold.

Minutes later they were out the door, barely remembering to lock it behind them. They jumped into the Jeep, and Flynn took off out of the driveway somehow managing to keep all four tires planted on the ground. The windows were rolled down, and they both attempted to decipher from what part of the town the sirens were coming from.

"There's never been two people taken in two consecutive days has there?" Jaime asked craning her neck out the open window. "You think we made a mistake last night? Pissed the demon off, maybe?"

"I haven't found any cases in consecutive days," Flynn responded as he maneuvered the Jeep around a corner near downtown. No sirens here. "But that doesn't mean it couldn't happen. Imagine how many disappearances were never reported over the years. Plus, the demon wasn't technically working on its own free will last night. It's got to be a possibility at least."

"Shit," Jaime exhaled. "Maybe there was more to the Settlement signing than we knew. There might have been some special ritual or chant Jared was supposed to say when he signed his name. We might have royally fucked this town and everyone in it."

Flynn kept quiet, not wanting to admit that she was probably right. Something must have gone wrong at some point last night. As Flynn replayed last night's events, he recalled telling Jared they would be by later that morning.

"Hey, let's swing by Jared's place and pick him up," Flynn threw out. "Guess we need to keep him in the loop with all of this. Then we can figure out where the sirens went to."

"I'd call him to wake him up, but we both seemed to have left our phones behind in our rush to get out the door."

"Shit," Flynn responded as he spun the wheel and turned the Jeep towards Jared's. "Let's hope he's up already. I really don't want to have to break into another –"

Suddenly, the sight of police cars and an ambulance on the street they had just turned on to severed his train of thought.

"Oh fuck," Jaime's voice was a whisper. "Fuck. What the fuck happened?"

The sirens of the police cruisers and the ambulance had been turned off, but the lights still blared in the morning sun.

"Jaime," Flynn choked out. "Jaime, that's Jared's house."

Everything suddenly seemed to move in slow motion. Jaime felt Flynn come to a stop almost half a block down from where the emergency vehicles were. She felt him shift into park, and then open and slam his door. She forced herself into action, despite her feet feeling like they were filled with cement. Her heart beat hard enough that she was sure Flynn could hear it, and her breath came short in broken gasps. Jaime felt herself slipping into a panic attack, but there was nothing she could do to stop it right now. She'd have to ride it out.

She met Flynn at the front of the Jeep, and they both paused to look up the street at where Jared's house sat. The front door was wide open, and there were several police officers, including Uncle Danny, standing in and around the yard. The back door of the ambulance was also open, and the gurney inside was gone.

Well, that's weird, Jaime thought. Why do they have the gurney out if there's no body? Hell, why is the ambulance even here to begin with? The simple answer came to her like a slap in the face. But it couldn't be, it didn't make any sense.

Caution tape had been strung up, blocking the property from the numerous gawkers who had made their way out of their homes. Flynn and Jaime approached the crowd, hoping to catch the eye of Uncle Danny. He was currently standing just outside the front door speaking with another one of his officers. From their position, they could see the gray and solemn lines of Uncle Danny's face. Once he was finished with the other officer, Uncle Danny turned to head back down the walkway towards one of the squad cars. He spotted Jaime and Flynn at the back of the group of people on the sidewalk. He raised a hand in greeting, but his face stayed the same. If anything, seeing them made his face become even more grim.

Uncle Danny was now standing at the driver's side of his squad car talking into his radio. They couldn't hear what he was saying from their position, but they could tell it was not a pleasant conversation.

"Do you have any idea what happened here?" Jaime had turned to the lady she was standing next to. She was wearing bright blue track pants with a matching zip-up jacket. Her pink t-shirt underneath read, '**Save Water. Drink Wine.**' On her feet were white tennis shoes that had probably never seen a tennis court. Jaime pegged her immediately as a soccer mom. She was familiar to Jaime, but she couldn't for the life of her remember the woman's name at the moment.

Soccer Mom shook her head no and shrugged her shoulders.

"I just got back from dropping my kids off at school," she explained. Her arms were crossed in front of her body, and she was gripping each elbow like they were her lifelines.

"I had just pulled back in a few doors down when I heard the sirens. I turned and there were the cop cars and ambulance. They all went rushing up and into the house, and then nothing. There was no screaming, no gunshots, nothing. I, of course, stayed where I was, and ducked down behind my minivan to see what was happening. Couple of minutes later, one of the officers is out putting up that tape, and then they're all just kind of standing around like they are now."

Jaime knew what all of that meant. Jared was dead inside that house. But if the demon came back to take him, why was his body still there? Did someone else kill Jared after he got home last night? Were they already in the house when they dropped him off last night?

Soccer Mom was still talking, but Jaime had zoned out thinking about someone lurking inside Jared's house while they were parked outside. Jaime couldn't help the shiver that ran up her spine.

"I'm sorry, what did you say?"

Soccer Mom shot her a sympathetic look, and then repeated herself.

"I said, that's the man whose wife went missing the other week. Did you know them?"

Jaime paused before answering. Sure, she knew them when they were all fourteen. When she was sure that her and Amber would end up at the same college, and they'd stay up all night studying for midterms and dreaming about their future. She knew them when they were sixteen, and Jared embarrassed her in front of her entire English class. She wished so badly she could just have disappeared for the rest of that day. She knew them when they were eighteen, and they had just graduated high school. Their little class of eighty-six people all crowded together in the gymnasium, grinning from ear to ear, everyone with big plans for the coming months.

"I went to high school with them." Jaime finally answered. "I knew them pretty well back then, but we kind of drifted apart over the years."

Soccer Mom nodded.

"That's how it always goes," she sympathized. "High school friends, a lot of the time, will drift apart down the road due to no fault on either side. Life just gets in the way."

Jaime opened her mouth to respond when she noticed Flynn was walking towards her. She hadn't even realized that he wasn't standing next to her anymore. She politely excused herself from Soccer Mom, and made her way over to meet him. His face now mirrored his uncle's, gloomy and upset.

"My uncle can't talk here, but he said to meet him back at the station."

Here, Flynn paused to run a hand through his hair and blow out a puff of air.

"He said it's bad, Jaime."

"He's dead, isn't he?"

Instead of answering right away, Flynn looked down at the ground as if his feet had suddenly become the most interesting things in the world. When he looked back up, tears were welling up in his eyes threatening to fall.

"Yeah," he managed to get out. "Yeah. He's dead, but my uncle didn't give any details of what happened. Let's hear what he has to tell us before we make any crazy decisions."

Jaime nodded in agreement, not trusting herself to speak. She had spent most of her life hating Jared and everything he did to her, but now she found herself mourning his death, a death she may or may not have been partially responsible for.

They trudged back to the Jeep and drove over to the police station to wait for Uncle Danny to return and inform them of the circumstances surrounding Jared's death.

Jaime, thankfully, hadn't made any other visits to the police station in the years between seeing the demon for the first time and the present day, and it hadn't changed much since

Jaime burst through its front doors fifteen years prior. The front desk was still in the same spot, and Jaime was even pretty sure the cop who sat behind the desk was the same one whom she had nearly given a heart attack to. He was fifteen years older, and probably twenty pounds heavier, but it was definitely the same guy. Lewis. The name popped into her head as if he was an old friend. His name was Lewis, and he had thought she was having a mental breakdown that night. Her and Flynn plopped themselves down in two of the chairs that sat in the front lobby and tried to make themselves comfortable.

"The last time I was here," Jaime began, trying to lighten the mood. "My parents were convinced that I was high on LSD or drunk on cheap beer. One of the cops actually brought out a breathalyzer test, after I finished telling what happened to me that night. Kind of weird that we'd end up back here, after all these years."

"I'll take you for some more ice cream once this is all over," Flynn tried to joke. The tears had subsided for the moment, but his face was red from rubbing his hands over it.

They were both still weary from the previous night, and this new twist in the story really seemed to wipe them out. All they wanted was to head back to Flynn's and crash for another couple of hours. The way the morning was heading, however, gave no indication they'd be doing that anytime soon.

"Do you think someone else knew about Chris and the demon? A partner?" Jaime thought out loud. "Maybe they followed us, saw what happened in the woods, and went after Jared out of revenge? And that they're looking for us now?"

Flynn became rigid in his chair. His eyes darted from the door of the station to Lewis sitting behind the desk. It'd take a lot of skill and not to mention a lot of guts to ambush two people sitting in the police station, but Flynn had seen stranger things happen these last few days. He was about to voice his opinion on the matter, when the door to the station swung open, and the they both rose slightly out of their chairs preparing to either run or fight. Instead of a hail of bullets raining down on them, Uncle Danny stepped through the doors and turned to them. His face was tired and worn. He tried to smile in greeting, but the smile never reached his eyes, and made the action look more like a grimace than a welcoming gesture.

"Come on," he croaked. "Let's go back into my office. We can talk there."

He led them past the front desk, past Lewis, and through the archway into the back squad room. There were five more desks back here that the officers all shared amongst each other. Uncle Danny, however, had his own office. On the job for almost twenty-five years now, he had worked his way up the short ladder so to speak, and that came with some small perks. He didn't go out on as many calls as he once did, but today had been different. He had been the one to take the phone call early that morning.

"Have a seat you two." Uncle Danny extended a hand in the direction of the two chairs that sat on the one side of his desk. He, himself, plopped down in his ergonomic, orthopedic chair on the opposite side and closed his eyes for a few seconds. "It's been a long morning and it's not even nine yet."

They both nodded, but remained silent waiting for him to be ready to tell them what happened that morning at Jared's house. They were anxious to know if they needed to be worried about someone possibly cutting the brake lines in their cars or hiding in their closets at home. Finally, Uncle Danny opened his eyes, and leaned forward and rested his elbows on his tidy desk. He looked first at his nephew, and then at Jaime.

"We got a call early this morning, right before eight." Uncle Danny spoke slowly and deliberately. It was how he had always talked, like a cop. Uncle Danny never made someone feel stupid when he talked to them, but he always made sure they understood what he was saying.

"I just happened to be the only one around at that moment, so I took the call. At first, there was nothing. I repeated myself, Hawk Ridge Police Department, please state your emergency, and still nothing. I waited almost a minute and a half, thinking someone had butt dialed the station. We get that about twice a week, and then someone finally started to talk."

"It's going to be a beautiful day today." came the male voice.

"Is there an emergency where you are, sir?" Uncle Danny questioned. He was a little worried how the voice sounded.

"Not yet. I'm just admiring how beautiful this town is when there's not so much ugly hiding underneath it."

"Sir, is there someone in the room with you? What is your current location? Are you able to tell me?" Uncle Danny kept his voice calm, not wanting to send the caller into a frantic state, but he needed to get him talking.

"No, it's not that. I'm alone," the voice answered, growing stronger. "I'm all alone in my house now. I don't have anyone to blame for that but myself."

"Okay. What's your name son? What are your plans for the day? You're right. It is going to be a beautiful day out."

At this point, Uncle Danny had an idea what was going on with this young man. He had once attended a negotiating seminar in Philadelphia one summer. A senior detective of the Philadelphia police department had told the attendees about a call he received that was very similar to the one he was currently fielding. He grabbed his radio and relayed to his other officers that he was going to need paramedics ready to go when he got the location of a caller, and for any free officers to standby.

"My name?" He sounded surprised. "My name is Jared McCloskey. What's your name, officer?"

"My name is Danny Baygo," he responded. McCloskey, he thought. Shit. This is the guy whose wife just went missing.

"Baygo," he repeated, trying out the sound of the name on his tongue. "Are you Flynn's father?"

"I'm his uncle. You went to school with him?" and then into his radio. "I need the paramedics at the McCloskey residence. 2642 Maple Ave. I need all available officers on scene. We have a 10-56A in progress."

The address came to the front of Uncle Danny's mind as his own address would. The disappearance of Amber McCloskey had been the talk of the town ever since it happened. They had had officers on scene at the house every other day it seemed, asking questions, looking for leads, and just giving updates to her husband, the now caller on the phone. He had always been Uncle Danny's lead suspect, call it a gut feeling, but they couldn't prove a damn thing. He had been on the football field when she was last seen, and therefore had an airtight alibi. A hitman, then, Uncle Danny had thought. But up until now, they hadn't been able to find any kind of paper trail, or anything on Jared's phone or computer. The phone call he was now having, however, was giving Uncle Danny the idea that he had been on the right track the whole time.

"Jared," he spoke into the phone. "Jared, I have some people coming over to see you. Do you think you can let them in the house when they get there?"

There was a long pause on the other end, and Uncle Danny's heart leapt into his throat. Finally, Jared came back on the line, although his voice was now very distraught.

"I can leave the door unlocked for them. I'll be inside in the kitchen. I need to go now,

Officer Danny. Thank you for listening to me." Here, he paused once more. "Your nephew is a really good guy. I wish I would have been better to him and Jaime when we were in high school."

"Jared!" he called into the receiver. "Jared! I need you to stay on the phone with me until my friends get there!"

But the line had already gone dead. Jared was gone. He tried to call back a few times, but it went straight to voicemail. He had either turned the phone off, or smashed it.

"Shit!" Uncle Danny screamed into the empty squad room. He slammed down the receiver back into its cradle and took off out the door, hoping that someone was already on scene.

"By the time the first officers on scene arrived, they were already too late," Uncle Danny lamented to his two listeners. "They banged on the door but there was no answer.

Helen moved around the side of the house trying to see in a window, and when she got to the one that looked into to the kitchen, that was when she called to get the door open and get inside."

"Carl tried the front door, and as Jared had said, it had been left unlocked. He was in the kitchen, just like he had told me. There's several exposed beams in the downstairs of that house. The one that runs through the kitchen is the one that young man hung himself from."

Twenty-Six

It was as though the air had been sucked out of Uncle Danny's office when he uttered those words. Hung himself. That had to be a mistake, Jaime thought. The idea that Jared would take his own life never even crossed her mind.

"You're absolutely sure that he did it himself?" Flynn asked. His voice was shaking and full of disbelief. "There was no sign of foul play?"

"I shouldn't be discussing this with anyone until the full investigation concludes, but I don't think I have to worry about you two blabbing to the whole town. As far as we could tell, it was a suicide. There was blood on the rope, on the knot where it was tied, on his phone we found on the floor, and all over his hands. No sign of any struggle, besides the chair that was kicked over. He had some bruising on his arms and his head, but they were already hours old when we arrived."

He paused, and mulled over how to continue.

"There was also a note. In it Jared explained how he and Chris Gallagher orchestrated Amber's disappearance."

Jaime was thankful that they were sitting down because all of a sudden, she couldn't feel her legs.

"He also explains that he got rid of Chris last night. That would explain all the bruises he had."

"Can we see it? The note?" Flynn asked in a watery voice.

"It's being logged in evidence right now, so I can't let you see it even if I wanted to. Like I said, he confesses that he and Gallagher got rid of Amber, and then says he got rid of Chris after they fought last night. He goes on to say that nobody will ever find the bodies."

"So he killed himself out of guilt?" Jaime theorized.

"I thought so at first, but then I read the rest of the note. There was one other thing in there," Uncle Danny added. His face was pained, and looked like he was struggling whether or not to tell them what was in the note.

Jaime and Flynn's foreheads broke out in a sheen of sweat. Flynn swallowed hard, and Jaime ground her teeth together in order to keep her composure under control. Were their names mentioned in it? Are they now suspects in Jared's death and the two disappearances?

"It said, 'I'm sorry for whatever happens to the town because of this, but I cannot let the cycle continue any longer.' And then he signed his name."

The office went completely still. Jaime and Flynn tried to keep their faces even, masking the emotions they were currently feeling. He didn't do it out of guilt, they both realized silently. He did it so that there would be no name on the Settlement. He did it so that no more families would have to live with an unknown fate of a loved one.

"It'll be twenty-five years at the end of the year that I've been a police officer in this town," Uncle Danny explained. "This is the first suicide I've seen in this town over that period. We haven't had a homicide in this town, in God knows how long. No bank robberies, no car jackings, and barely any thefts. What we have had over the years is missing person's reports. People from this town just seem to vanish into thin air. I'm even beginning to think that the Millsap kid is just a straight up vanishing act."

"After noticing an increase in our missing person's reports this year, I began doing a little digging. I went back to our last missing person's report, and discovered it was fifteen years ago. The same year you busted through those front doors after coming from Amber's house, Jaime."

Hearing this, Jaime sat unmoving. She was sure in that moment, he was about to accuse her of having something to do with Amber's disappearance.

"I kept digging. I wanted to see how often these missing persons popped up, and if there was any kind of pattern so to speak. Fifteen years, like clockwork, people would go missing from town, never to be heard from again. I still have no idea what it was that scared you so bad you felt you had to come here instead of going home that night. And I certainly have no idea what you two have been up to with Jared lately. I know for a fact, the two of you hated his guts in high school."

At this, their eyes widened. Uncle Danny cleared his throat before continuing.

"I also know that you two had nothing to do with Jared's death this morning."

This last part he added, when he saw their eyes grow wide. He struggled to finish his thoughts. He was torn between wanting to know what had been happening in his town, and wanting to just send them away and never have them speak of it again. He was still fighting with his next words when Jaime broke in.

"We're still not entirely sure about everything that has been going on in Hawk Ridge over the last two hundred and odd years. We're not even sure anything is going to change. But, I think that if people do stop going missing in fifteen years, other things are going to start happening in this town instead."

Uncle Danny considered what she had said. Finally, he nodded his head in understanding.

"We'll cross that bridge when we come to it. No use worrying about any of that now, when this town is going to be mourning two of its football coaches. Two men it thought it could trust with its sons. The backlash from this is going to be immense once word gets out, but least Amber's parents will have some closure now."

Closure was a strong word, Jaime thought. They would never really know the truth about what happened to their daughter. They would never have a body to bury, or even cremate. She guessed they would just have to look to their God to find what it was they wanted.

The office fell into an uncomfortable silence, no one quite sure what to say. Finally,

Uncle Danny stated that he needed to get back to work, and get over to the hospital over in Crawford. That was where they had taken Jared's body for the time being. He told them to take as much time as they needed in the office. Jaime and Flynn thanked him for talking with them, and bid their farewells for the time being. Once Uncle Danny had vacated the office, the pair turned to one another, eyes wide, and mouths hung open.

"Now what?" Jaime sputtered. "We go home and pretend none of this ever happened?"

"We both know that's never going to happen," Flynn countered. "I'm guessing that the demon took enough sacrifices this year for the town to have another prosperous fifteen years, but after that? Who knows. All we can do right now is wait."

Jaime leaned forward resting her elbows on her knees, and gripped her head between her hands.

"Getting rid of the demon was supposed to make me feel better." Her voice came out small and muffled voice. "I think I feel worse now than I did fifteen years ago."

Flynn reached over and placed a comforting hand in the middle of her back. He had no idea what to say to make things better. He never could have imagined this is how everything would turn out.

"Let's go home," he finally settled on. "We haven't had nearly enough coffee this morning to deal with something of this magnitude."

Jaime gave a small chuckle as they stood up to leave the office. Outside, there wasn't a cloud in the sky. The sun was in full effect, and the air held a crispness one could only find during the fall season. They had to admit that Jared had been right, it was going to be a beautiful day.

Back at the house, the pair dragged themselves up the front walk. They still couldn't get over how fast everything had occurred over the past week. Suddenly, Jaime came to a halt at the foot of the stairs leading up to the front porch. Flynn bumped into the back of her, and barely managed to keep the two of them from tumbling forward onto their faces.

"Hey! What gives?" Flynn asked a little annoyed. He just wanted to get in the house and get a fresh pot of coffee brewing.

Jaime stood where she was for a few seconds longer and then lunged forward. She scrambled up the steps and dove to her knees in front of the welcome mat.

"Jaime?" Flynn called, concern evident in his voice.

She ignored him as she pulled something out from underneath the welcome mat. An envelope. On the front were three words scribbled in haphazard writing. *Jaime and Flynn.*

"What the hell?" Flynn had made his way up on the porch, and was crouched down next to Jaime.

Without thinking, Jaime ripped open the envelope and pulled out the piece of paper that was inside. With shaking hands, she unfolded the paper and more of the wobbly handwriting came into view.

Guys,

By the time you find this, I'll be gone. Please don't feel guilty over my death. This is the only way to make sure the demon doesn't come back in fifteen years. At least, I hope so. Guess you'll have to wait and see for sure. Anyway, thank you for helping me. I know that you didn't have to, and I definitely didn't deserve it. You're both better persons than I ever would have been. This town is lucky to have you guys, even if after all of this you leave and never come back. Maybe, hopefully, I'll see you guys on the other side. Until then, keep kicking it in the ass.

-Jared.

They read through the letter twice, three times, before either of them could speak again.

"He must have snuck over here while we were still asleep," Jaime squeaked out. "The son of a bitch knew what he was going to do probably as soon as he signed that Settlement last night."

"As soon as we dropped him off at home he must have went inside, wrote this, and then made his way over here to leave it on the porch." Flynn concluded in disbelief. "We were so focused on finding the sirens earlier, that we never noticed it sitting right here in front of our faces."

"He makes it sound like it'll be so easy to get over. Like we just lost a football game or something. Get back in the weight room, watch some film, try again harder next game."

Flynn shook his head. Whether it was in disbelief or anger, Jaime didn't know. She, herself, didn't know how to feel. She was still in shock, and yes, she was angry, but she also couldn't help but feel something that she couldn't pinpoint. Had this been fifteen years ago, she believed whole heartedly that Jared never would have put anyone else's well-being ahead of his own. Was this pride? Could one feel pride for someone who had just killed themselves? Jaime wasn't sure, and it was making her head throb just thinking about it.

After several more minutes of re-reading the note, Flynn tore himself away from it and climbed to his feet. He reached down and offered Jaime a hand, pulling her to her still unsteady legs. When he went to tug her inside the house, however, she pulled back.

"You go start the coffee," she explained to his confused look. "I'll be right in. Just want a couple more minutes of fresh air."

Flynn offered a small smile and a nod in return. He then turned and disappeared through the front door, and Jaime was alone. She moved to stand against the railing of the porch, and leaned down so that her forearms rested flat against the top rail. She looked out over the street that she had spent so much time on as a kid. She had rollerbladed with Flynn and played kickball with the other neighborhood kids. She even broke her wrist once diving into home, aka the manhole cover, trying to avoid the tag. Everything was just as she left it seven years ago, almost as if it was waiting for her return.

Nothing ever changes in this town, she thought for probably the hundredth time since coming home. Except, that wasn't exactly true. Sure, all the businesses downtown were still the same, the football team still sucked, and everyone still loved them despite that. But Jared was proof that the people of this town could and did change. Jaime felt tears sting the back of her eyes at this thought, and instead of pushing them back, she let one fall. And then another, and another.

She didn't blubber or sob; she just let the tears she had been holding back for so long finally fall. She cried for Amber, her first love and up to now, her only love. She cried for who they could have been together, and for who Amber had become. She cried for Gary Kinkaid. A man whose life had been turned upside down one night in 1957, and had stayed that way since. She cried for Jared. He had had no clue what he was getting himself into when he went to Chris. Not that that absolved him from the role he played in Amber's disappearance. Hell no. Jaime still hated him for that. But his ultimate sacrifice, she couldn't stop thinking about that. And finally, she cried for the town. The next fifteen years would probably be okay, but after that? Would things finally start to change in Hawk Ridge? She didn't know, and didn't want to spend any time thinking about it. What will be, will be her mom always said.

Twenty-Seven

March 2018 – Pennsylvania

The back door of the U-Haul truck slid shut with a bang, and the handle was locked into place. The next morning it would be off on its seven and a half hour journey north.

"You sure about this?"

"Little late for that now, don't you think?" Flynn joked.

Jaime smiled in return. She was beyond excited that Flynn was finally getting out of this town, and was moving north to Maine with her. The last several months included four trips to Maine for Flynn filled with job and house hunting. His last trip in February was strictly to sign his new employment papers with a general contractor based in Portland. The owner had been impressed with Flynn's work experience for his age, and the fact that Flynn had been helping his dad run his business since he was in high school. He was also currently going through the process of buying a two-bedroom, two bath house in Saco. They were set to close on the house that coming weekend if all went according to plan.

  When Flynn had originally sat down back in October and told his parents that he would not only be selling his childhood home, but also moving out of state, they had not been as supportive as he had hoped. His mom cried and his dad was furious, but as time went on, and they realized that he was going to go through with it no matter what, they both came around to the idea, for the most part, of him starting a new chapter of his life.

  The last few months for Jaime had been strange to say the least. Part of her felt lighter as though she had finally closed a section of her life that had hung over her like a black cloud.

She still had nightmares every so often, but at least now she wasn't terrified she was going to open her eyes and see antlers looming over her in bed. She had also made peace with the fact that she was never going to see Amber again. Sure, she wished every day that she could go back and redo their last interaction, but there was nothing she could change now. She was moving on from Amber, but she also wanted to keep a part of her tucked down deep inside. After all, she did have some pretty good memories with her that she wanted to hold on to.

The 'true' mystery of Amber's disappearance had been put out in the Herald. They had published a story explaining that Jared and she had had an argument that night after the scrimmage, and he killed her. The article goes on to say how he and his fellow football coach, Chris Gallagher, disposed of her body. Where the body ultimately ended up the paper didn't know, and didn't speculate, and for that Jaime was relieved. They had their confession letter, and that was good enough for them. At least Amber's parents, along with the town, could have some kind of closure. Although, once the town learned that two of its beloved football coaches murdered and disposed of Jared's wife, the bleachers on Friday nights that season were considerably more vacant.

On this night that was to be Flynn's last in Hawk Ridge for the foreseeable future, both his and Jaime's parents were getting together at Flynn's parents' house for a cookout and a sort of going away party. The U-Haul was currently parked at the Strait residence since Flynn had since sold his house to a couple who had been a few grades below them in school. The couple were good people, and Flynn was confident they would treat the place with love and respect.

Flynn would drive the U-haul and Jaime, who had flown down from Maine this time around, would lead in the Jeep.

"Hey," Flynn pulled her out of her daydream. "You still with me?"

"Yeah, just thinking about the last time I came home. You still having nightmares?"

His sudden aversion to meet her eyes gave her all the answer she needed. She wanted to tell him that it would get better and easier, that the nightmares would eventually go away, and that he wouldn't wake up tangled in the sheets drenched in sweat forever. But, they both knew it was going to be a long time before either of them got over their experiences in Hawk Ridge.

"Come on," Flynn said trying to change the subject. "There's somewhere I know you've been wanting to go visit."

The Hawk Ridge cemetery was located near the town line. It dated back to the founding of the town, just like everything else. One could find headstones in there that were so old the names were completely worn off. Jaime and Flynn wove their way through the countless rows. Thankfully, Flynn knew where he was going since he had been here for the burial. In fact, he was the only person at the burial.

Grass hadn't begun to grow yet on the small plot of ground where they eventually came to a stop. Its resident had been cremated and then buried in a plain wooden box. The marker was much less elaborate than the other ones in the surrounding rows. Jaime glanced around and realized that this must have been the area of the cemetery for those who didn't have anyone to pay for a giant gravestone.

"I'm glad that we could at least make the last few months of his life a little more comfortable than it had been in years," Jaime said looking down at the marker.

GARY CHARLES KINKAID

JUNE 4TH, 1936 – OCTOBER 13TH, 2017

"After you went back to Maine, I gave him a call and asked if I could come see him again. That afternoon, I showed up and we sat for hours. He listened in silence as I told him everything. The only time he interrupted was when I told him the contract was in the trophy case instead of the historical society. He claimed he would've figure it out himself had he been twenty years younger."

"I have no doubt about that," Jaime added. "He did a lot of our work for us."

Flynn nodded and then continued.

"After all that, I told him about Jared's suicide and the note he left for the police. He was quiet for a long time once I finished speaking. Then out of nowhere, he started to cry. I just sat there and watched as he cried these chest heaving sobs. I think he had been holding it all in for the past sixty years, and finally just let it all out. Once he got himself under control again, he thanked me for all we had done. Said he was finally at peace with the fact he hadn't been hallucinating all those years ago."

"I wish I could have been here for the funeral," Jaime lamented. "But I'm glad he at least had you there."

The pair stood in silence listening to the wind whip around them. Finally, Jaime elbowed Flynn and motioned that they needed to get going. They made their way back out to the Jeep, suddenly wanting to be out of the cemetery.

"So what do you say?" Flynn asked as he turned the ignition and pointed the Jeep in the direction of his parents' house. "Think we'll be coming back for Christmas every year?"

Jaime thought it over, tilting her head back and forth. She still wasn't a huge fan of the town, or of a lot of the people in it. But despite all that, whenever someone asked her where she was from her answer was Hawk Ridge, Pennsylvania. This is what all those country songs she hated so much were all about. This was home.

Twenty-Eight

Somewhere, USA – Twenty years later

"There's no way this will work," The voice was skeptical. It was distinctly female, and it was shaking with nerves.

She wasn't sure that they should have been out here in the dark. It was almost springtime, but the temperatures at night were still dropping down to freezing. If they made one wrong turn trying to get home, even with the full moon, they'd be lost for good. She didn't even know if their father, who had spent his entire life in these woods could track them down.

"The website I found a few months ago claimed it would," a second voice, male this time. He was much more eager than his counterpart to be doing whatever it was they were doing. "It gave specific instructions. There were several people who claimed it had worked for them."

"What do we do if he shows up?" The girl asked. Excitement was finally starting to creep into her voice. "What is he supposed to look like, anyway?"

"We tell him what we want, what we need, what our family needs." Her brother replied as he finished covering something in the ground with the shovel they had brought with them. "I think he can appear as different things. Someone in Mexico posted that he came to them as a giant black goat. Someone else in Australia said he was a red dragon. My guess is that he can come to someone as whatever he wants."

He finished, and then looked around where they were standing. The box was in the ground, inside was everything the online thread had told him to put in it. If this didn't save the family farm, he wasn't sure anything could.

The wind whipped the tree branches against one another, creating a squeaking and scratching sound that made them both clench their teeth. The two siblings huddled together against the cold under a large pine tree. They stood there for what felt like hours until they couldn't feel their toes any longer. Just when they were about to admit defeat, they heard a raspy voice speak up from behind them. It startled them enough to drop the shovel, and let out two identical shrieks. It was clearly a man's voice, deep and guttural. But it also held a welcoming tone. As if whoever was standing behind them just wanted to help them, or give them some candy.

"I spy, with my little eye," came the growl. "Some naughty, naughty children."

The siblings, wrought with fear, rotated themselves around to see who or what had joined them. They were terrified of what kind of creature they might discover standing behind them. When they finally made the full rotation, and could now see their new 'friend'. They almost sighed in relief at the sight. Leaning up against a towering pine tree, illuminated by the full moon was a man in a black suit. His black hair was slicked back with grease that shone in the moonlight, and his goatee was perfectly trimmed and shaped. His lips were drawn back in a smile that revealed two rows of straight, bone white teeth. He looked like a businessman getting ready to make a sale. He looked perfectly normal, like any man you might see on the streets, except that his eyes glowed a sickly shade of yellow.

"You, you can help us?" the boy managed to squeak out. "You can help our family?"

"That depends," the man snarled, still grinning. "On what it is you're willing to offer me."

Acknowledgements

I owe the creation and publication of this book to the efforts of a number of individuals. Many thanks to the following people:

To my 9th grade English teacher, Ms. Jodie Andrefski, the first person to tell me I had a talent and should pursue creative writing. Your kind and encouraging words resonated with 14-year-old me, and have stuck ever since.

To my other three high school English teachers, Mr. Dennis Vavra, Mr. Kieren Cray, and Mrs. Nicole Zakrewsky. Thank you for allowing me to stretch my wings on all your essays, writing prompts, research projects, and presentations.

To my 7th grade Geography teacher, Mrs. Sara Karnish, thank you for always discussing *SURVIVOR* with me during class time, and your continued friendship over the years. I hope your current students know how lucky they are to have you.

To Miki Bennett, for giving me the best advice I've ever received about writing, and giving me the final push I needed to sit down, write something, and get it published.

To my editor, Kimberle Unger, for her valued edits, input, and advice. She took a lot of my rookie mistakes, and helped me turn it into something I'm very proud of. Any and all mistakes you find in this book are my own, not Kim's.

To Brandon Lueder, for offering to read an early draft of this book and adding his own helpful insight.

To James Wylder for answering all of my questions about publishing, and to his girlfriend, one of my good friends, Rebecca Jacob, for introducing us.

To my mom and dad, for always encouraging and supporting my love of reading and writing, and all things weird. And also for letting me watch *The X-Files* when I was 9.

To my brother, Matt Rupert, the Sam Winchester to my Dean Winchester. Thanks for always having my back, Bitch.

To my partner, my best friend, and the best thing to ever happen to me, Kacie Marcus. Thank you for continuously reminding me that it would all be worth it someday, and for always being the voice of reason when my mind jumps to the worst possible outcome. And most importantly, for believing in me when I don't believe in myself. I love you, Nugget.

About the Author

Deanne Rupert grew up on a steady diet of *Goosebumps, Scary Stories to Tell in the Dark,* and the *Cirque du Freak* series. After spending years writing down ideas for books in notebooks, on her phone, and on her laptop, Deanne finally got serious and finished her debut novel, *To Live Without Knowing.*

Deanne is originally from Barnesville, Pennsylvania, and currently resides in Summerville, South Carolina, with her girlfriend, Kacie, and their Staffordshire Bull Terrier, Jones.

You can follow Deanne on Twitter, @Dee_Wexler or Instagram, @drupert313